A World in Focus

A UNIQUE TEXT FOR SOCIAL STUDIES

Text: Elaine Pascoe
Editorial Advisor: John-Paul Bianchi

NORTH AMERICA

BLACKBIRCH PRESS, INC. STATE ST. SCHOOL

WOODBRIDGE, CONNECTICUT

Published by Blackbirch Press, Inc.
260 Amity Road
Woodbridge, CT 06525

Web site: www.blackbirch.com
Email: staff@blackbirch.com

©2000 Blackbirch Press, Inc.
First Edition

Printed in the United States

10 9 8 7 6 5 4 3 2 1

Photo Credits
Cover (top and bottom left); back cover (bottom left and right), pages 4, 6, 8 (top left and right), 10 (left), 29 (top), 47 (top left), 58 (top), 67 (right), 68 (left center and bottom right), 69, 70 (bottom), 78-80, 83-87 (top right and middle left), 89-91 (top left and right), 92: Corel Corporation; cover (top center and right; right center and bottom; left center); back cover (top; bottom center); pages 8 (bottom), 12, 14, 16 (top), 17 (top), 18 (top left), 20 (bottom right), 21-22, 24-27 (bottom), 31 (bottom), 32, 34, 36-38 (top and center right), 39 (top and bottom right), 41, 44 (bottom), 46, 48 (top), 49 (bottom), 50, 52, 54 (top left and right), 55 (bottom), 57-58 (bottom), 60-63 (bottom), 65-67 (bottom), 68, 70 (top right), 72: PhotoDisc; pages 9 (top), 10 (top; center right), 11 (bottom), page 16 (center), 20 (top left), 27 (top left), 29 (bottom right), 30 (top left), 38 (bottom), 39 (top left), 44 (middle left), 47 (bottom right), 54 (bottom right), 56, 63, 81, 88 (bottom right): Library of Congress; page 9 (bottom): The Rhode Island Historical Society; page 11 (top): National Park Service, Nez Percé National Historical Park, E.G. Gustavensen; pages 17 (center), 48, 55 (top), 64: Blackbirch Press, Inc.; pages 18 (top right), 28, 75: North Wind Picture Archives; page 18 (bottom): Buffalo and Erie County Historical Society; page 19 (top): Rhode Island Tourism Division; page 19 (bottom): The New-York Historical Society, New York City; page 20 (center right): The State of New Jersey; pages 30 (right), 70 (top left): National Archives; page 49 (top): United States Department of the Interior Bureau of Reclamation; page 73: PhotoSpin; page 74: National Portrait Gallery; page 77: Vic Boswell/Collection of the Supreme Court of the United States; pages 87 (bottom), 88, 91 (bottom right): Mexican Government Tourist Office.

Library of Congress Cataloging-in-Publication Data
Pascoe, Elaine.
   A World in Focus : North America / by Elaine Pascoe.
     p.   cm.
Includes index.
   ISBN 1-56711-345-1 (pbk. : alk. paper)
   1. North America—Geography—Juvenile literature. 2. North America—History—Juvenile literature.
[1. North America.] I. Title.

E40.5 .P37 2000
970—dc21

00-010307
CIP
AC

Table of Contents

North America

Introduction

You're about to tour the third largest of the world's seven **continents**—North America. North America stretches over more than 9 million square miles of territory. Only Asia and Africa have more land. Three large countries share most of this vast continent. Canada is in the North, Mexico is in the South, and the United States is in the middle.

The Grand Canyon

These countries have much in common. Long before their boundaries were drawn, Native Americans lived here. Later, Europeans founded **colonies** throughout North America. The United States, Canada, and Mexico all started out as colonies of European countries. All three nations won their independence, each in its own way and time. Today all three nations have **democratic systems** of government. People choose their government officials by voting in elections.

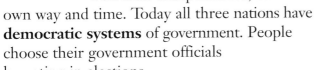

Inuit woman

Canada, Mexico, and the United States share a landscape that has almost every possible feature. There are snow-covered mountain peaks and rolling plains. There are mighty rivers and huge freshwater lakes. These features help make North America beautiful. The continent's eastern coasts face the Atlantic Ocean and Europe. Its western coasts face the Pacific Ocean and Asia. That has helped the nations of North America build trade links with countries all over the world.

North America also has every kind of climate. There are steamy **rain forests** in southern Mexico. Off the northern coasts of Canada and Alaska, the ocean is frozen

Girl from Miami, Florida

for most of the year. Most places in North America have the type of climate that is called **temperate**. Summers are warm, and winters are cool or cold.

Today, most people in North America live in and around cities. Two of the world's five largest cities—Mexico City and New York—are in North America. The continent still has plenty of wide-open spaces, but population growth has created problems, such as pollution. Those problems are another thing that the countries of North America share.

Despite the common threads, each part of North America has qualities that make it a special place. In this book, you will read about the first people of North America. You'll also learn about the foundations of the American democratic system. You'll tour the continent, visiting six major regions of the United States—the Northeast, the South, the Midwest, the Mountain States, the Southwest, and the Pacific States. You'll also tour Canada and Mexico.

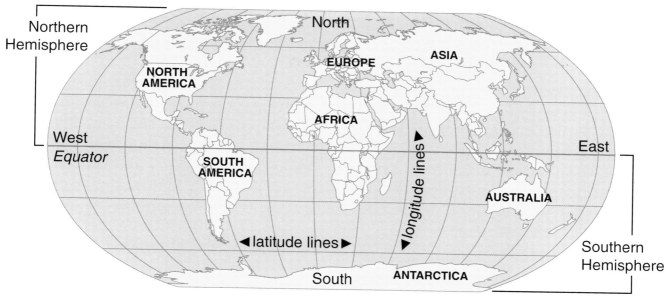

The World of Maps

What is the highest point in Alaska? Where are Brazil's minerals located? What is the capital of Mexico? Where do most people in Canada live? The answers to all these questions can be found on maps.

A map is a carefully drawn picture of the earth or a part of the earth. Maps are important tools that give us all kinds of information. There are maps of your city, your state, your country, and your planet. There are even maps of the moon and maps of the ocean floor. A **topographical map** would help you find the highest point in Alaska. It shows natural features—jungles, deserts, and mountains. Look at a **natural resources map** to locate Brazil's minerals. To find the capital of Mexico you would check a **political map**. It shows you capital cities, big cities, and the borders between countries. If you looked at a **population density map** you would see where most people in Canada live.

Maps can answer lots of questions, but you have to know how to read them. There are four important **direction** words on a map. **North** is the direction toward the North Pole. It is shown at the top of the map. **South** is toward the South Pole. It is shown at the bottom of the map. **East** is the direction where the sun rises each morning. It's on the right side of the map. **West** is the direction where the sun sets each evening. It's on the left side of the map. Most maps have a **compass** that shows these four directions.

You will see the word **equator** on most world maps. The equator is an imaginary line around the fat, middle part of the earth. It divides the earth into two equal parts. The **Northern Hemisphere** is above the equator. The **Southern Hemisphere** is below the equator. Many other imaginary lines appear on a map. Lines of **latitude** go around the world in the same direction as the equator (from left to right). You can tell how far north or south a place is by looking at them. Lines of **longitude** go around the world from the North Pole to the South Pole (from top to bottom). They can tell you how far east or west a place is.

The **map key** helps you understand the information you see on a map. On most maps a circle or dot indicates a major city. A star usually shows the location of a country's capital.

The blue areas are water. More than 70% of the earth's surface is covered by water. The Atlantic Ocean, the Pacific Ocean, the Indian Ocean, and the Arctic Ocean are earth's major bodies of water. These oceans separate huge land masses called continents. The seven continents are Asia, Africa, North America, South America, Antarctica, Europe, and Australia.

The First Americans

Who were the first Americans? Where did they come from? No one knows for certain. But **archaeologists**—people who study the remains of ancient civilizations—have some ideas.

The most widely held idea is that people first came to North America from Asia. During the last stage of the Ice Age—20,000 years ago and more—huge **glaciers** covered much of the Northern Hemisphere. So much of the world's water was frozen in these huge sheets of ice that sea levels were much lower than they are today. The Bering Strait, between Alaska and Siberia, was drained dry. Thus Asia and North America were linked by a **land bridge**. Ice Age animals—mammoths, huge bison, giant deer—roamed across the bridge. So did hunters who followed the herds.

About 12,500 years ago, the glaciers began to retreat. That opened the way for people to migrate from Alaska throughout North America. These wanderers are known as the Clovis people, for stone knives and spear points that were found near Clovis, New Mexico. Similar stone tools have been found across most of North America and in South America. They show that by 10,000 B.C. people were living in most parts of the Americas.

The Clovis people are believed to be ancestors of today's Native Americans. But they may not have been the first people in the Americas. Recently, archaeologists have found evidence that other people may have reached parts of North and South America thousands of years earlier. These people may have come by different routes, from several parts of the world. The question of who the first Americans were remains a mystery.

ANCIENT CITIES AND EMPIRES

America's earliest people left few records, but archaeologists have pieced together enough information to give a picture of how they lived. As the glaciers shrank, North America's climate warmed. Many of the Ice-Age animals hunted by the Clovis people died out. People hunted smaller game, fished, and gathered wild nuts and plants. In time, they began to grow crops.

Remains of an ancient temple.

Indians who lived in what is now central Mexico were the first to grow corn, squash, and beans. They were clearing fields and planting crops around 7000 B.C. Slowly, this knowledge spread. Farming changed the way people lived. Instead of moving from place to place to hunt and gather food, they settled in villages in places where crops could be grown. Villages grew into towns. These changes took place at different times in different places. Where food was scarce and the soil was poor, change came later.

Where farming was especially successful, complex societies developed. Over centuries,

YOUNG EXPLORER

Can you find the Yucatan Peninsula on the map (page 7)?

KEY
- Arctic
- Subarctic
- Northwest Coast
- California
- Plateau
- Great Basin
- Southwest
- Great Plains
- Northeast and Great Lakes
- Southeast
- Middle America

[tribe] = ancient peoples

North American Tribes About 1500

cities and empires rose, flourished, and fell. The people who built them disappeared—sometimes mysteriously. New groups rose to take their place, often carrying on customs of the earlier groups. Most of these early societies were ruled by kings and priests. In some, slavery and human sacrifice were part of life. The ancient cities were also places where arts and crafts flourished.

Pyramid Builders

Mexico was the site of some of the earliest and greatest Indian civilizations. The Olmec were thriving there by 800 B.C. Olmec cities had pyramids, ceremonial courtyards, and stone platforms where temples and other public buildings may have stood. Around the cities were **irrigated** fields. The Olmec also carved sculptures,

Mayan Pyramid of the Magician   Huge stone serpent head carved by the Olmec

first, their villages were simple. But over generations, they became skilled stonemasons. By 900, they were building stone **pueblos**—multifamily dwellings something like today's apartment houses. The most spectacular of these, like the Cliff Palace at Mesa Verde, in Colorado, were carved into the sides of sheer cliffs. Some had hundreds of rooms.

including gigantic stone heads that may have honored their kings.

The Olmec Indians traded with other groups, and their art and culture spread. This set a pattern and model for later civilizations in Mexico. These included Mayan cities, on the Yucatan Peninsula, and Teotihuacan, near present-day Mexico City. By A.D. 1500, the Aztecs had become the most powerful people in Mexico. In their capital city, Tenochtitlan, canals linked temples, palaces, and markets.

The Anasazi flourished for hundreds of years, but in the 1200s they abandoned their cliff dwellings. A long drought made it impossible for them to grow crops. They left the region, abandoning tools, pottery, and even clothing.

Pueblo Builders

About 2,000 years ago, towns began to appear in what are today Arizona and New Mexico. The Hohokum, who lived there, traded with the people of Mexico. Their towns were a lot like those in Mexico at the time, with pyramid-like mounds and courts where ceremonial ball games were played. Like the early people of Mexico, the Hohokum also built irrigation systems.

The Anasazi were living in what is now the American Southwest by A.D. 500. At

Anasazi cliff dwellings

Mound Builders

Farther east, in what is today the central United States, the Adena and Hopewell people lived. These people built earth mounds as fortifications, as tombs, and for religious reasons that aren't well understood today. Some of the Adena mounds are in the shapes of birds or serpents. The Hopewell people included several distinct groups. Some were fine weavers, and others were artisans who made beautiful copper ornaments. They traded with other Indian groups as far away as Canada and Florida.

People known as the Mississipians replaced the Hopewell people by around 800 B.C. Like the Hopewell people, the

Mississippians were mound builders. Their largest city, Cahokia, was on the eastern shore of the Mississippi River, opposite present-day St. Louis, Missouri. At its center was a huge mound, 100 feet tall, with a flat area the size of a football field on top. Temples probably once stood there. Other mounds and platforms were arranged around the central mound. As many as 20,000 people may have lived in this city at its peak, in the 1100s. Cahokia and most other ancient Mississipian sites were abandoned before Europeans arrived in the 1500s.

MANY NATIONS

How many people lived in America when Europeans arrived? Historians think there were anywhere from 2.5 million to more than 20 million in what is today the United States, excluding Alaska. These people included many separate groups, each with its own customs. There were some similarities among the groups, however.

Most Native Americans depended on a mixture of hunting, gathering, and farming. Women often took charge of farming and preparing food, while men hunted. Men were also warriors. Women as well as men played important roles in making community decisions. **Clans**, or groups of related families, were the basis of many Indian societies. Groups traded with one another over surprising distances—given that roads, wheels, and horses were unknown.

American Indians lived in harmony with the natural world. Nature also played an important part in their religious beliefs. A few tribes used a sort of symbol writing, similar to Egyptian hieroglyphics, for important records. But, for the most part, they had an oral tradition, handing down stories from one generation to the next.

The Eastern Woodlands

Many Eastern Woodlands Indians lived in small villages. Their homes were made of wood, with sheets of bark covering the roofs. Some villages were surrounded by palisades, walls

Seneca chief

of pointed stakes. Corn, beans, and squash were grown in fields around the village. Men hunted deer and other forest animals, or they fished along the coast.

Many of the eastern Indians spoke Algonkian languages. These groups included the Micmac, Mahican, Narragansett, Powhatan, Shawnee, and Natchez. Southeastern nations included the Cherokee, Creek, Choctaw, and Chickasaw.

Powwow of Narragansett Indians

The Iroquois, members of a different language group, lived along the present-day U.S.–Canadian border and in upstate New York. The Five Nations of the Iroquois—the Mohawk, Oneida, Onondaga, Cayuga, and Seneca—formed a powerful alliance to oppose other tribes in the region, chiefly the Huron. The Iroquois were also known for their longhouses, in which many members of a clan lived together.

The Plains

The life of Indians on the Plains was linked to the huge herds of bison that once roamed the prairies. The bison provided meat, and their hides were used for clothing and shelter. Dried meat and hides were also traded for other essential items.

Bison of North America

Some groups spent the entire year hunting, moving from place to place to follow the bison herds. They included the Blackfoot, Shoshoni, Comanche, and Kiowa. The Cheyenne, Arapaho, and Sioux tribes originally lived in farming villages and took long hunting trips. Eventually they gave up their villages to live year-round on the Plains. Other groups farmed in the valleys of the Missouri and other rivers. Out on the prairies there was not enough rain to grow corn. Only root crops, such as wild carrots, turnips, and camas, could survive.

Top: Blackfoot tipis
Above: Pueblo houses

The Plains Indians were the first to ride horses. Horses came to the southern prairies with Spanish explorers and settlers. Some of these horses escaped or were stolen. By the mid-1700s, all the Plains nations had horses. They used them for hunting, war, and as pack animals.

The Far West

Deserts and mountains made life a challenge for many Indians of the Far West. In the harshest lands, people lived in small groups wherever there was enough water to grow crops. In river valleys, where corn, beans, and squash could be grown, larger villages sprang up.

In the Southwest, the Pueblo nations—the Hopi, Zuni, and others—carried on the tradition of pueblo building begun by the Anasazi. Scattered among the Pueblo settlements were villages of the Apache and

 Think About It

Why did horses become important to the Plains Indians?

Navajo, who moved into this region from the northern plains.

The Mohave, western Paiute, and other groups of the western deserts and mountains often moved from camp to camp in search of food. They grew root crops, hunted rabbits and other game, and fished in mountain streams. They were expert basket weavers, and many of their baskets are considered works of art.

The Pomo and other Indians of California lived in villages. They harvested grains from native grasses that thrived in the dry climate and acorns, which they ground into a flour.

The Northwest

Fish—especially salmon—and other sources of food were plentiful in the Pacific Northwest. There were permanent villages here as early as 1000 B.C. In time, this area became the center of a trade network. The Columbia River linked interior tribes—the Yakima, Walla Walla, Nez Percé, and others—to coastal groups. These included the Chinook, at the mouth of the river; the Bella Coola, Squamish, and Kwakiutl, in what is today British Columbia; and the Haida and Tlingit, along the coast as far north as Alaska.

The Pacific Northwest nations became famous for their art and culture. Homes were long wooden houses shared by several related families. The houses were richly decorated with paintings and carvings. Totem poles— tall poles carved with likenesses of the clan's heroes and guiding spirits—stood outside. Legends and history were celebrated in dances and dramatic performances. Another Northwest custom was the potlatch, a community feast held to celebrate important events. The hosts of a potlatch went all out, showering guests with food and lavish gifts, to show their generosity.

Nez Percé powwow, 1901

The Far North

The forests of Canada and Alaska were home to many Indian groups, from the Cree in the east to the Kaska and Tanana in the west. Along the coasts of the Bering Sea and Arctic Ocean lived the Inuit (Eskimo), Yupik, and Aleut peoples. They thrived in the face of harsh conditions. Winter brought months of bitter cold, ice, and snow.

The Inuit hunted caribou and went to sea in boats called umiaks to spear whales. They paddled kayaks in pursuit of seals and other ocean animals. Hunting provided them with almost everything they needed, from meat to skins for clothing. Inuit homes were solid round structures, built of sod or, sometimes, ice blocks. Families sheltered in coastal villages during the long winters. In the short summers, they often traveled

Totem poles in Nimkish village.

from camp to camp, fishing, hunting, and gathering berries.

EUROPEANS ARRIVE

Norse sailors are thought to have been the first Europeans to arrive in North America, around A.D. 1000. Europeans didn't come in large numbers for more than 500 years, after Christopher Columbus made his famous voyage of discovery in 1492. During the 16th century, explorers and traders from England, France, Russia, Spain, and other lands made contact with many Indian groups.

Contact with Europeans had a major effect on the Indians. In Mexico, the Aztec Empire fell to Spanish conquest in 1521. Elsewhere, trade brought some benefits at first. By trading furs, Indians obtained guns, iron knives and pots, and other European goods. The competition for trade often led to conflicts among Indian groups.

Fur traders were followed by European settlers. The Indians had much to teach the first settlers. For example, Indians showed the settlers how to grow corn, which wasn't

Think About It

Why did the Inuit live by hunting rather than farming?

grown in Europe. As settlers began to take up more land, they left less land for the Native Americans. This led to increased conflicts and wars. Almost 350 English settlers were killed in an Indian uprising in Virginia in 1622. Fifteen years later, the Pequot War in Massachusetts all but wiped out the Pequot tribe. The pattern was repeated in many conflicts that followed. Over the next 250 years, as settlers spread across the continent, Indians were pushed back.

Even worse for the Indians were the diseases such as smallpox, that the colonists brought with them. The Indians had no natural immunity to these diseases, which sometimes wiped out entire villages. White settlers brought other changes. Farms, towns, and roads carved up Native American hunting grounds. The great bison herds died out in the 1800s, ending the Plains tribes' way of life.

FOCUS ON: Native American Words

More than 2,000 English words are based on Native American words. Many of these words refer to plants, animals, and places that were new to European colonists. Here are some of them:

bayou	potato
chipmunk	raccoon
hickory	savanna
hominy	skunk
hurricane	squash
moose	tobacco
opossum	tomato
pecan	yucca

Many American place names are also based on Indian names. Among them are the names of 24 states:

Alabama	Mississippi
Alaska	Missouri
Arizona	Nebraska
Arkansas	North Dakota
Connecticut	Ohio
Illinois	Oklahoma
Iowa	South Dakota
Kansas	Tennessee
Kentucky	Texas
Massachusetts	Utah
Michigan	Wisconsin
Minnesota	Wyoming

FOCUS ON: "The Trail of Tears"

Many southeastern Indian nations adapted to the arrival of white settlers in their homeland. By the early 1800s their farms and businesses were thriving. Among whites, the Cherokee, Creek, Seminole, Choctaw, the Chickasaw became known as the "Five Civilized Tribes."

In 1830, U.S. President Andrew Jackson signed the Removal Act. Under this law, the U.S. government could force Indians to trade land in settled states for unsettled land in the western territories. Most members of the Five Civilized Tribes, as well as Indians in areas such as Ohio and the Great Lakes region, were turned off their land. They were forced to march hundreds of miles to Oklahoma, where they had to clear land and build new homes. Many died from hardships on the long march. Today the route they traveled is known as "The Trail of Tears."

The U.S. census of 1890 recorded 250,000 Indians, a small fraction of the number present when Europeans first arrived. Most were living in poverty on government reservations. Since then, the Indian population has grown again, to about 2 million. Native Americans today take pride in their heritage. They have more opportunities for jobs and education than their grandparents did. The long conflict between Indians and whites will always be one of the most troubling chapters in American history.

CHAPTER REVIEW

1. During the Ice Age, a land bridge connected what two regions?
2. Who were the Clovis people?
3. When did Indians farm in Mexico?
4. Where did the Olmec live?
5. What type of dwellings did the Anasazi build?
6. What were the Five Nations of the Iroquois?
7. What was a potatch?
8. Who were most likely the first Europeans to reach North America?
9. Why were European diseases such as smallpox disastrous for Indians?
10. How many Native Americans lived in the United States in 1890? How many today?

Activities

Here is a list of 12 people who played an important part in Native American history. Choose one for a short report. Tell what your subject did and why he or she is important. You might wish to use the Internet for some of your research.

JOSEPH BRANDT (THAYENDANEGEA), Mohawk
COCHISE, Apache
GERONIMO (GOYATHLAY), Apache
HIAWATHA, Mohawk
CHIEF JOSEPH, Nez Percé
OSCEOLA, Seminole
POCAHONTAS, Powhatan
PONTIAC, Ottawa
RED CLOUD (MAKHPIYA LUTA), Lakota Sioux
SACAGAWEA, Shoshoni
SEQUOYA, Cherokee
TECUMSEH, Shawnee

The Northeast

 Imagine that you are aboard the space shuttle, looking down on the northeastern United States. What do you see? From that great height, rolling hills and mountains give the land a crumpled look. Rivers, streams, and lakes are splattered everywhere. To the east, the Atlantic Ocean pounds a coastline cut by many bays and inlets. To the north and west are Lake Ontario and Lake Erie, two of North America's Great Lakes. Forests and fields cover some of the land. This region also has some of the nation's biggest and oldest cities, and its suburbs are home to millions of people.

Nine states make up the region we call the Northeast. They include the six New England states: Maine, New Hampshire, Vermont, Massachusetts, Connecticut, and Rhode Island. New York, New Jersey, and Pennsylvania complete the group.

THE LAND

The hills and mountains of the Northeast form part of the Appalachian Highlands. This is a broad region that stretches from Canada south into Alabama. The northern part of this region includes the

Maine lighthouse built on the rocky shore.

White Mountains in Maine and New Hampshire, the Green Mountains in Vermont, the Adirondacks in New York, and the Allegheny Mountains in Pennsylvania. Mount Washington, in New Hampshire, is the highest peak in the Northeast at 6,288 feet.

South from Cape Cod, a narrow coastal plain borders the Atlantic Ocean. Deep bays and inlets along the Northeast coast provide many natural harbors. In colonial days, these harbors played a key role in the settlement of the region. So did the many rivers and streams that flow from the hills toward the ocean. The Hudson

 **AT A GLANCE**

The Northeastern States

 ## Connecticut
Area: 5,018 sq mi (12,997 km2)
Capital: Hartford
Statehood: January 9, 1788;
the 5th state
State motto: *Qui transtulit sustinet*
(He who transplanted sustains).
Nickname: Constitution State;
Nutmeg State
Abbreviations: CT, Conn.
State bird: American robin
State flower:
Mountain laurel
State tree:
White oak

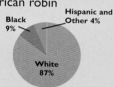
Black 9%
Hispanic and Other 4%
White 87%

 ## Maine
Area: 33,265 sq mi (86,156 km2)
Capital: Augusta
Statehood: March 15, 1820;
the 23rd state
State motto: *Dirigo* (I lead).
Nickname: Pine Tree State
Abbreviations: ME, Me.
State bird: Chickadee
State flower:
Eastern white
pinecone and
tassel
State tree:
Eastern white pine

Hispanic and Other 2%
White 98%

 ## New Hampshire
Area: 9,279 sq mi (24,932 km2)
Capital: Concord
Statehood: June 21, 1788;
the 9th state
State motto: "Live free or die."
Nickname: Granite state
Abbreviations: NH, N.H.
State bird:
Purple finch
State flower:
Purple lilac
State tree:
White birch

Hispanic and Other 2%
White 98%

 ## New Jersey
Area: 7,787 sq mi (20,169 km2)
Capital: Trenton
Statehood: December 18, 1787;
the 3rd state
State motto: "Liberty and
prosperity"
Nickname: Garden State
Abbreviations: NJ, N.J.
State bird:
Eastern
goldfinch
State flower:
Purple violet
State tree:
Red oak

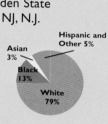
Asian 3%
Hispanic and Other 5%
Black 13%
White 79%

 ## New York
Area: 49,108 sq mi (127,189 km2)
Capital: Albany
Statehood: July 26, 1788;
the 11th state
State motto: *Excelsior* (Ever
upward).
Nickname: Empire State
Abbreviations: NY; N.Y.
State bird:
Bluebird
State flower:
Rose
State tree:
Sugar maple

Asian 3%
Hispanic and Other 11%
Black 14%
White 72%

 ## Pennsylvania
Area: 45,308 sq mi (117,348 km2)
Capital: Harrisburg
Statehood: December 12, 1787;
the 2nd state
State motto: "Virtue, liberty, and
independence"
Nickname: Keystone State;
Quaker State
Abbreviations: PA, Penn.
State bird:
Ruffed grouse
State flower:
Mountain laurel
State tree:
Eastern hemlock

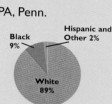
Black 9%
Hispanic and Other 2%
White 89%

 ## Rhode Island
Area: 1,212 sq mi (3,140 km2)
Capital: Providence
Statehood: May 29, 1790;
the 13th state
State motto: "Hope"
Nickname: Ocean State
Abbreviations: RI, R.I.
State bird:
Rhode Island
Red chicken
State flower:
Violet
State tree: Red
maple

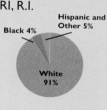
Black 4%
Hispanic and Other 5%
White 91%

 ## Massachusetts
Area: 8,284 sq mi (21,456 km2)
Capital: Boston
Statehood: February 6, 1788;
the 6th state
State motto: *Ense petit placidam
sub libertate quietem* (By the sword
we seek peace, but peace only under
liberty).
Nickname: Bay State
Abbreviations: MA, Mass.
State bird:
Chickadee
State flower:
Mayflower
State tree:
American elm

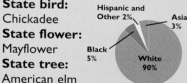
Hispanic and Other 2%
Asian 3%
Black 5%
White 90%

 ## Vermont
Area: 9,614 sq mi (24,900 km2)
Capital: Montpelier
Statehood: March 4, 1791;
the 14th state
State motto: "Freedom and unity"
Nickname: Green Mountain State
Abbreviations: VT, Vt.
State bird:
Hermit thrush
State flower:
Red clover
State tree:
Sugar maple

Hispanic and Other 2%
White 98%

Cape Cod, Massachusetts is a popular vacation spot.

and Delaware rivers, in New York and New Jersey, are among the most important. Other major rivers are the Susquehanna, in Pennsylvania, and the Kennebec, Merrimack, and Connecticut in New England.

Originally, much of this region was covered with stands of white pine, hemlock, beech, sugar maple, and other forest trees. The forests were filled with white-tailed deer, wild turkeys, raccoons, and even panthers and black bears. Those ancient forests are gone—and so are the panthers. But many areas are wooded, especially in the mountains. Bears, deer, turkeys, and many other wild animals still live in this part of the United States.

New Englanders have a saying: "If you don't like the weather, just wait a minute." Changeable weather is a fact of life through-out the Northeast, not just in New England. Temperatures vary widely from day to day and from season to season. Summers are

Samuel de Champlain, founder of Quebec

warm, and winters are often cold and snowy. Glorious fall foliage brings many tourists to the Northeast.

Generally, the northern part of the region has longer winters and cooler temperatures in all seasons. Other factors, such as nearness to the ocean or the mountains, influence the weather. A weather station on Mount Washington in New Hampshire has recorded some of the nation's coldest temperatures and the strongest winds.

EUROPEANS ARRIVE

English, French, and Dutch explorers visited the Northeast in the 1500s and 1600s. Giovanni da Verrazano and Jacques Cartier explored the Atlantic coast in the 1500s. Henry Hudson sailed up the Hudson River in 1609. Samuel de Champlain entered the New York region from Canada at about the same time.

The explorers were searching for riches or fast routes to Asia. Many of the early European settlers also came in search of religious freedom. English settlers known as the Pilgrims sailed the Atlantic on the *Mayflower*. They founded the first permanent colony at Plymouth, Massachusetts, in 1620. They had broken away from the Church of England. In America, they hoped to find a place where

Think About It

Why do you think the first European explorers visited the Northeast first?

The Mayflower at Plymouth, Massachusetts.

settled in New Sweden, on the Delaware River. Their colony was later taken over by the Dutch. In 1664, England took control of all the Dutch holdings in North America. New Amsterdam became New York City.

EARLY DAYS

The early settlers cleared much of the land for farming and cut more of the forest for timber. In most areas, they found that soils were not very **fertile**. Especially in New England, the hilly, rocky land made farming difficult. For those reasons, farms in the Northeast tended to be small, compared to those in other parts of the country. Farmers dug stones from the ground and set them on the edges of their fields, creating "stone fences." These stone walls still mark the landscape in many areas.

they could worship as they saw fit. Soon, they joined with the Puritans, another break-away group. Together, they founded the Massachusetts Bay Colony, centered in Boston.

The Puritan church controlled daily life and religious thought in the colony. That eventually led some settlers to leave and found new settlements of their own. Rhode Island, Connecticut, and New Hampshire were all founded by settlers who left Massachusetts. Pennsylvania became known as a place where people of all religions were welcome. Its founder, William Penn, was a member of the religious group known as the Quakers.

Not all the Northeast's early settlers were searching for religious freedom, and they were not all from England. Dutch traders established New Holland, which included most of what is today New York and New Jersey. New Amsterdam, on Manhattan Island at the mouth of the Hudson River, was the main Dutch settlement. Swedes

William Penn, founder of Pennsylvania

The Northeast's long coastline and many harbors offered other ways for people to make a living. Shipbuilding was an important industry. By the time of the Revolutionary War in 1775, American shipyards were building about a third of Britain's ships. Into the 1800s, fishing and whaling were also very important. From ports at Mystic, Connecticut, and Nantucket and

YOUNG EXPLORER

Can you find Massachusetts on the map (page 14)?

Why do you think whaling ships set sail from this area?

Old whaling ship in Mystic, Connecticut.

The fight on Lexington Common, April 19, 1775.

New Bedford, Massachusetts, whaling ships set out on voyages that lasted for years.

Harbors and rivers also helped the Northeast become a center for trade. Rivers provided natural highways for carrying goods from inland regions to the coast. From there, ships set out for ports around the world. Some of the first Europeans in the region came to trade with Indians for furs. Later, goods of all kinds passed through New York, Boston, and other ports. Ships from the Northeast also played a role in the slave trade, bringing slaves from Africa.

Patriots from the Northeast played a leading role in the struggle for independence from Britain. The shots that started the Revolutionary War in 1775 were fired at Lexington and Concord, Massachusetts. Many of the war's key battles were fought in the region.

After independence, new industries began to spring up. The Northeast's rushing streams turned waterwheels that powered textile mills and other factories. During the 1800s, farming became less important in the Northeast, while manufacturing and trade grew.

CITIES GROW

One reason for the decline of farming was the opening of the Erie Canal, in 1825. The canal linked the Hudson River in New York to the Great Lakes. This allowed products to be shipped from the Midwest, where soils were more fertile. Many farmers packed up and headed west, setting up new farms there. Others left their farms for factory work. Many young women also found work in factories in the 1800s. This gave them a degree of independence that was rare for the time.

Mule teams pulling the canal boats, Erie Canal.

YOUNG EXPLORER

Can you find Boston, New York City, and Providence on the map (page 14)?

What do these important cities have in common?

Focus On: Slater Mill

Pawtucket, Rhode Island, is sometimes called the "cradle" of the Industrial Revolution in America. It was here that Samuel Slater set up America's first successful textile mill, in 1790. The machines at the mill manufactured cotton and were powered by a waterwheel. Slater Mill National Historic Site preserves the original mill and a later mill, along with early machinery.

Slater Mill

As manufacturing and trade grew, so did cities. Along the coast, Boston and New York City remained the largest ports. New York grew especially fast. Its location at the mouth of the Hudson River made it the nation's most important center for trade and finance. By the mid-1800s, it was the nation's largest city.

In New England, cities such as Fall River and Lowell, Massachusetts, grew up around textile mills. Elsewhere factories turned out shoes, clocks, guns, and all kinds of other products. In Pennsylvania and New Jersey, iron-making became a major industry. Beginning in the mid-1800s, new manufacturing methods allowed steel to be made in great quantity and at low cost for the first time. Bethlehem and Pittsburgh, Pennsylvania, were among the centers of the new steel industry. Coal mining and, later, chemical manufacturing also became important.

The shift from farming to manufacturing brought major changes to daily life. On the farm, life revolved around the seasons. Families grew most of

Workers forging steel in Pittsburgh around 1886.

their own food and made most of their own clothes, furniture, and other needs. In cities, life revolved around the whistles that announced the start and end of work shifts in the factories. Workers used their wages to buy their food and other needs. The wages were low, the work was hard, and the hours were long.

Men and women from the Northeast were among the leaders of reform movements that sought to right social wrongs. Topping the list of those wrongs was slavery. Beginning in the 1830s, William Lloyd Garrison and others led the **abolitionist** movement, which sought to end slavery. Many Northeasterners helped slaves to escape to Canada by means of the "Underground Railway." The slavery issue was finally settled by the Civil War. After the war's end in 1865, reformers took up other causes. Some worked to gain the vote for women. Others worked to improve life for growing numbers of poor people in the nation's many cities.

Immigrants on the S.S. Patricia, 1906.

NEW ARRIVALS

In colonial times, most people in the Northeast were English from the British Isles. Smaller numbers were Dutch, German, French, or Scandinavian. Beginning in the 1800s, people poured into the Northeast from many lands. Some were passing through, on their way to the West. Many others stayed and found work in the urban factories, shipyards, and construction projects. Their numbers helped the population of the cities swell.

The Irish were the biggest **immigrant** group in the years before the Civil War. After the war, Italians, Poles, Portuguese, Germans, and Slavs arrived in large numbers. Each of these groups eventually became part of the region's lively **ethnic** mixture, even though they often faced discrimination at first. New immigrants usually got the lowest paying jobs and the worst housing in the cities.

After the Civil War, many African Americans also moved to Northeastern cities. Like immigrants from other lands, they hoped to find better working conditions, jobs, and a better way of life. They also faced discrimination. While immigrants from Europe were generally accepted in time, African Americans continued to struggle against prejudice. Despite their struggles, they, too, helped bring the region into the modern era.

THE NORTHEAST TODAY

Today, people from Asia, Latin America, Africa, and the Caribbean have joined the earlier immigrants to the Northeast.

Atlantic City, New Jersey, has many hotels and casinos.

Focus On: Ellis Island

From 1892 to 1954, 12 million immigrants entered the United States at Ellis Island, in New York Harbor. They sailed past the gleaming Statue of Liberty on their way to the U.S. Immigration Station there. Today about 40 percent of Americans have at least one ancestor who landed at Ellis Island. The Ellis Island facility was restored in the 1980s and is now open as a museum.

Ellis Island Museum, New York City harbor

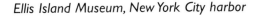

Statue of Liberty, New York City harbor   Independence Hall, Philadelphia   Waterfront, Boston

There have been many other changes, too. There are far fewer farms than there were in the 1800s. Better farming methods have made the remaining farms far more productive.

Many older industries, such as steel and textile manufacturing, have declined, but new ones have sprung up. People in the Northeast today work in many fields—health care, education, business services, wholesale and retail trade, transportation and communications—as well as manufacturing.

This **diversified** economy has brought general wealth, but pockets of poverty remain—especially in the cities.

The Northeast's cities have continued to grow, although more slowly than in the past.

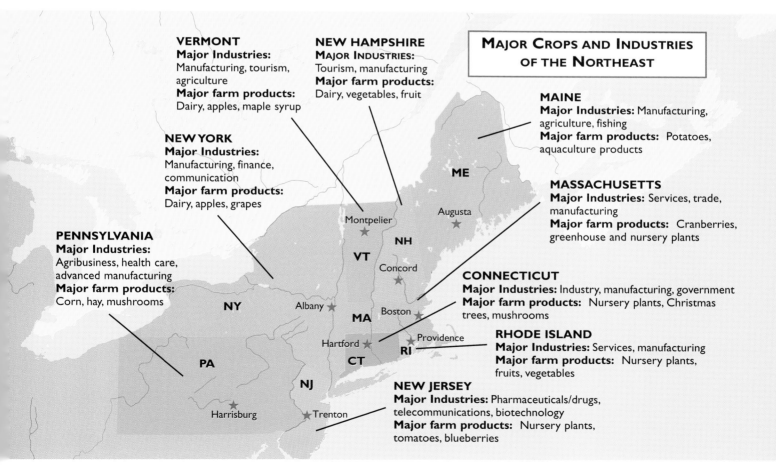

MAJOR CROPS AND INDUSTRIES OF THE NORTHEAST

VERMONT
Major Industries: Manufacturing, tourism, agriculture
Major farm products: Dairy, apples, maple syrup

NEW HAMPSHIRE
Major Industries: Tourism, manufacturing
Major farm products: Dairy, vegetables, fruit

MAINE
Major Industries: Manufacturing, agriculture, fishing
Major farm products: Potatoes, aquaculture products

NEW YORK
Major Industries: Manufacturing, finance, communication
Major farm products: Dairy, apples, grapes

MASSACHUSETTS
Major Industries: Services, trade, manufacturing
Major farm products: Cranberries, greenhouse and nursery plants

PENNSYLVANIA
Major Industries: Agribusiness, health care, advanced manufacturing
Major farm products: Corn, hay, mushrooms

CONNECTICUT
Major Industries: Industry, manufacturing, government
Major farm products: Nursery plants, Christmas trees, mushrooms

RHODE ISLAND
Major Industries: Services, manufacturing
Major farm products: Nursery plants, fruits, vegetables

NEW JERSEY
Major Industries: Pharmaceuticals/drugs, telecommunications, biotechnology
Major farm products: Nursery plants, tomatoes, blueberries

Montpelier · Augusta · Concord · Albany · Boston · Providence · Hartford · Harrisburg · Trenton

ME · NH · VT · NY · MA · RI · CT · PA · NJ

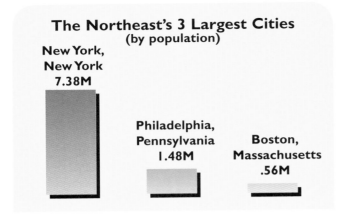

The Northeast's 3 Largest Cities
(by population)

New York,
New York
7.38M

Philadelphia,
Pennsylvania
1.48M

Boston,
Massachusetts
.56M

Covered bridge in New Hampshire.

Linked by highways, they have spread out into suburbs. A belt of cities and suburbs stretches almost unbroken from Boston in Massachusetts, through New York, New Jersey, and Pennsylvania. Shopping malls and drive-in restaurants make suburbs throughout the region seem much the same. Each city, however, has a unique character. Boston is known as a center for education, science, and art. New York, with its towering skyscrapers, is still the nation's financial capital. Stocks worth more than $1 trillion dollars change hands daily in the city's financial markets. Philadelphia is the nation's fifth-largest metropolitan area. Each year, millions of people visit its historic sites, including Independence Hall, where the Declaration of Independence was signed.

Beyond the city skylines and sprawling suburbs, the Northeast still has open land and forests. Many communities are taking steps to preserve and protect the natural environment. Parks, mountains, and beaches draw many visitors each year. So do the stately historic homes, village greens, and white-steepled churches that date back to colonial times. They are reminders of the Northeast's rich history.

CHAPTER REVIEW

1. Name one of the mountain ranges of the Northeast.
2. Rhode Island and Connecticut were founded by settlers who left what colony?
3. How did rivers help the Northeast become a center for trade?
4. What was one reason for the decline of farming in the Northeast during the 1800s?
5. What cities became centers of the steel industry?
6. What was the goal of the abolitionist movement?
7. What immigrant group was the largest before the Civil War?
8. Why are today's farms more productive than those of the past?
9. Which northeastern city is the nation's financial capital?
10. Name one of the attractions that draws visitors to the Northeast.

 Think About It

Can you think of things in the Northeast that take their names from other countries or languages? [Example: New York; York is a city/county in England]

Can you think of things in your region that have been named for or by one of America's ethnic groups?

Focus On: Celebrating the Northeast

Here is a partial list of the many festivals and special events celebrated by towns and cities in the Northeast. Choose one as the subject of a research paper. Then write about it in as much detail as possible.

CONNECTICUT
Schemitzun
September, North Stonington

MAINE
Downeast Country Dance Festival
March, Bath

MASSACHUSETTS
Boston Harborfest
June 28–July 4, Boston

NEW HAMPSHIRE
Great North Woods Lumberjack Championships
June, Berlin

NEW JERSEY
Delaware Bay Day Festival
June, Port Norris

NEW YORK
Three Kings Day Parade (Dedfille de los Tres Reyes)
January 6, New York City

PENNSYLVANIA
Revolutionary Times
September, Chadds Ford

RHODE ISLAND
Newport Music Festival
July, Newport

Activities

Here is a listing of some famous people who were born or lived in the Northeast. Choose a person as a topic for a brief research paper. Research your topic on the Internet and at your local library. Describe your subject's accomplishments and what was most significant about his or her life.

Connecticut
NATHAN HALE Hero of the American Revolution.
HARRIET BEECHER STOWE Abolitionist and author of *Uncle Tom's Cabin*.

Maine
HANNIBAL HAMLIN Senator, 15th Vice-President of the United States.
EDNA ST. VINCENT MILLAY Pulitzer Prize-winning poet and author.

Massachusetts
SUSAN B. ANTHONY Social reformer; led women's suffrage movement.
JOHN F. KENNEDY 35th President of the United States.

New Hampshire
MARY BAKER EDDY Founder of the Christian Scientist Church.
DANIEL WEBSTER Lawyer, statesman, orator.

New Jersey
AARON BURR U.S. Senator, Revolutionary War hero, third Vice-President of the United States.
GROVER CLEVELAND 22nd President of the United States.

New York
FRANKLIN DELANO ROOSEVELT Born in Hyde Park; 32nd President of the United States.
ELIZABETH CADY STANTON Organized the first women's rights convention; fought for women's suffrage.

Pennsylvania
JAMES BUCHANAN 15th President of the United States.
STEPHEN FOSTER Songwriter; most famous for song "Oh! Susanna."

Rhode Island
OLIVER HAZARD PERRY Naval officer; hero of the War of 1812.
GILBERT STUART Renowned portrait painter; most famous portraits of Washington, Adams, Jefferson, and Madison.

Vermont
CHESTER ALAN ARTHUR 21st President of the United States.
CALVIN COOLIDGE 30th President of the United States.

The South

USA

Equator

The South is known for its gentle climate, miles of sandy beaches, and a tradition of hospitality. Those features have placed parts of the South among the top vacation spots in the United States. The South has much more to offer. It's a lively and varied region, with farms and orchards, mist-shrouded mountains, and some of America's fastest-growing and most popular cities.

Fourteen states make up the South. They can be divided into three groups. Delaware, Maryland, Kentucky, and West Virginia are sometimes called the Border states. They lie along the border between North and South. Virginia, North Carolina, South Carolina, Georgia, and Florida are the Southeastern states. Tennessee, Alabama, Arkansas, Louisiana, and Mississippi make up the South Central group.

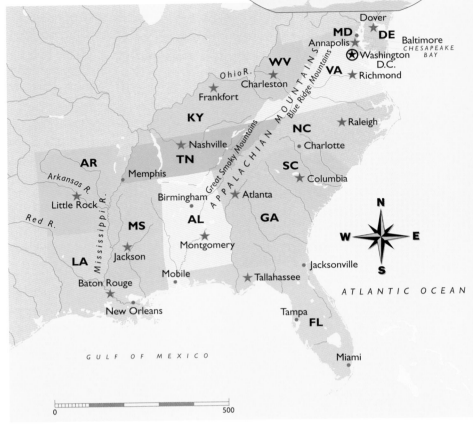

Cape Hatteras, North Carolina, is on a barrier island.

THE LAND

The coastline of the South stretches from Delaware, south around the tip of Florida, and west along the Gulf of Mexico. **Barrier islands**, sand dunes, and salt marshes rim the shores. Strong surf and shifting sandbars make stretches of the Atlantic coast treacherous for ships. In other places, deep bays provide safe harbors. The largest of these is Chesapeake Bay. It cuts north into Virginia and Maryland for about 200 miles.

Beyond the coast is a wide plain. Fertile soil here is ideal for farming. Farther west is the hilly Piedmont. This

 **AT A GLANCE**

The Southern States

 ALABAMA
Area: 50,750 sq mi (131,443 km2)
Capital: Montgomery
Statehood: December 14, 1819;
the 22nd state
State motto: *Audemus jura nostra defendere* (We dare defend our rights).
Nickname: Yellowhammer State
Abbreviations: AL, Ala.
State bird: Yellowhammer (flicker)
State flower: Camellia
State tree: Southern longleaf pine

Black 25%
Hispanic and Other 1%
White 74%

 ARKANSAS
Area: 52,075 sq mi (134,874 km2)
Capital: Little Rock
Statehood: June 15, 1836;
the 25th state
State motto: *Regnat populus* (The people rule).
Nickname: The Natural State
Abbreviations: AR, Ark.
State bird: Mockingbird
State flower: Apple blossom
State tree: Pine tree

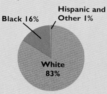
Black 16%
Hispanic and Other 1%
White 83%

 DELAWARE
Area: 2,044 sq mi (5,295 km2)
Capital: Dover
Statehood: December 1, 1787;
the 1st state
State motto: "Liberty and independence"
Nickname: First State
Abbreviations: DE, Del.
State bird: Blue hen chicken
State flower: Peach blossom
State tree: American holly

Black 17%
Hispanic and Other 3%
White 80%

 FLORIDA
Area: 53,997 sq mi (139,852 km2)
Capital: Tallahassee
Statehood: March 3, 1845;
the 27th state
State motto: "In God we trust."
Nickname: Sunshine State (1970)
Abbreviations: FL, Fla.
State bird: Mockingbird
State flower: Orange blossom
State tree: Sabal palm

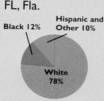
Black 12%
Hispanic and Other 10%
White 78%

 GEORGIA
Area: 57,919 sq mi (150,010 km2)
Capital: Atlanta
Statehood: January 2, 1788;
the 4th state
State motto: "Wisdom, justice, and moderation"
Nicknames: Peach State; Empire State of the South
Abbreviations: GA, Ga.
State bird: Brown thrasher
State flower: Cherokee rose
State tree: Live oak

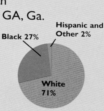
Black 27%
Hispanic and Other 2%
White 71%

 KENTUCKY
Area: 39,732 sq mi. (102,907 km2)
Capital: Frankfort
Statehood: June 1, 1792;
the 15th state
State motto: "United we stand, divided we fall."
Nickname: Bluegrass State
Abbreviations: KY, Ky.
State bird: Kentucky cardinal
State flower: Goldenrod
State tree: Tulip poplar

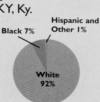
Black 7%
Hispanic and Other 1%
White 92%

 LOUISIANA
Area: 43,566 sq mi (112,836 km2)
Capital: Baton Rouge
Statehood: April 30, 1812;
the 18th state
State motto: "Union, justice, and confidence"
Nickname: Pelican State
Abbreviations: LA, La.
State bird: Eastern brown pelican
State flower: Magnolia
State tree: Bald cypress

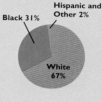
Black 31%
Hispanic and Other 2%
White 67%

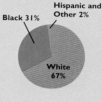 **MARYLAND**
Area: 9,775 sq mi (25,316 km2)
Capital: Annapolis
Statehood: April 28, 1788;
the 7th state
State motto: *Fatti maschii, parole femine* (Manly deeds, womanly words).
Nicknames: Free State; Old Line State
Abbreviations: MD, Md.
State bird: Baltimore oriole
State flower: Black-eyed susan
State tree: White oak

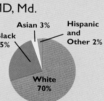
Asian 3%
Black 25%
Hispanic and Other 2%
White 70%

Baltimore, Maryland

MISSISSIPPI
Area: 46,914 sq mi (121,506 km2)
Capital: Jackson
Statehood: December 10, 1817; the 20th state
State motto: *Virtute et armis* (By valor and arms).
Nickname: Magnolia State
Abbreviations: MS, Miss.
State bird: Mockingbird
State flower: Magnolia blossom
State tree: Magnolia

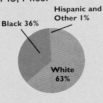

Black 36% — Hispanic and Other 1% — White 63%

NORTH CAROLINA
Area: 48,718 sq mi (126,180 km2)
Capital: Raleigh
Statehood: November 21, 1789; the 12th state
State motto: *Esse quam videri* (To be rather than to seem).
Nickname: Tar Heel State
Abbreviations: NC, N.C.
State bird: Cardinal
State flower: Dogwood
State tree: Pine tree

Native American 1% — Hispanic and Other 1% — Black 22% — White 76%

SOUTH CAROLINA
Area: 30,111 sq mi (77,988 km2)
Capital: Columbia
Statehood: May 23, 1788; the 8th state
State mottoes: *Animis opibusque parati* (Prepared in mind and resources) *and Dum spiro spero* (While I breathe, I hope).
Nickname: Palmetto State
Abbreviations: SC, S.C.
State bird: Carolina wren
State flower: Carolina yellow jessamine
State tree: Palmetto tree

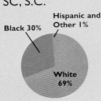

Black 30% — Hispanic and Other 1% — White 69%

TENNESSEE
Area: 41,220 sq mi (106,759 km2)
Capital: Nashville
Statehood: June 1, 1796; the 16th state
State motto: "Agriculture and Commerce" (1987)
Nickname: Volunteer State
Abbreviations: TN, Tenn.
State bird: Mockingbird
State flower: Iris
State tree: Tulip poplar

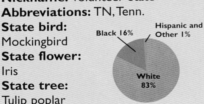

Black 16% — Hispanic and Other 1% — White 83%

VIRGINIA
Area: 39,598 sq mi (102,558 km2)
Capital: Richmond
Statehood: June 25, 1788; the 10th state
State motto: *Sic semper tyrannis* (Thus always to tyrants).
Nicknames: The Old Dominion; Mother of Presidents
Abbreviations: VA, Va.
State bird: Cardinal
State flower: Dogwood
State tree: Dogwood

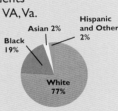

Asian 2% — Hispanic and Other 2% — Black 19% — White 77%

WEST VIRGINIA
Area: 24,087 sq mi (62,384 km2)
Capital: Charleston
Statehood: June 20, 1863; the 35th state
State motto: *Montani semper liberi* (Mountaineers are always free).
Nickname: Mountain State
Abbreviations: WV, W.Va.
State bird: Cardinal
State flower: Rhododendron
State tree: Sugar maple

Hispanic and Other 4% — White 96%

region's swift-running streams provided water power for the South's early industries.

From the Piedmont, the land rises steadily to the mountains. Several mountain ranges, all part of the Appalachian chain, run from Virginia to Alabama. They include the scenic Blue Ridge and Great Smoky mountains. From a distance,

Autumn colors in West Virginia.

the forested peaks seem to be shrouded in a blue haze.

Beyond the mountain ridges are uplands cut with valleys and **gorges**. In the early days of the United States, the South's major rivers were important routes for traders and settlers. The Ohio River winds along the north-western borders of West Virginia and

Hernando de Soto explored the Southeast from 1539 to 1542.

Kentucky. It joins the Mississippi, which flows through the heart of the South Central states to the Gulf of Mexico. Several major rivers flow into the Mississippi from the west. They include the Arkansas River and the Red River.

Coal and iron are among the South's greatest mineral resources. Oil is pumped from wells along the Gulf Coast. Pine forests provide timber, wood pulp for paper and products such as turpentine and resins.

The South's climate is generally mild and humid year-round. Winter brings freezing temperatures and even snow in the mountains, especially farther north. But the cold snaps seldom last long. Spring comes early, giving farmers a long growing season. Southern Florida enjoys year-round warmth.

Sun-starved vacationers flock there from the North each winter.

EUROPEANS ARRIVE

Spanish explorers arrived in the South in the 1500s. Juan Ponce de Leon was the first to reach Florida, in 1513. He was searching for the mythical Fountain of Youth. Hernando de Soto explored much of the Southeast from 1539 to 1542. The first European to reach the Mississippi River, de Soto fell ill and died there. In 1565, the Spanish founded St. Augustine, Florida. It was the first permanent European settlement in what would become the United States.

The first English colony in North America was Jamestown, founded in Virginia in 1607. Starvation, disease, Indian attacks, and quarrels nearly destroyed the little settlement during its first years. Virginians finally began to thrive after the English settlers turned to growing a new cash crop—tobacco.

Other English colonies were soon founded in the Southeast. Maryland welcomed Catholics, who were persecuted in Protestant England. In South Carolina, English settlers tried—and failed—to set up a system of hereditary nobility. Georgia, founded in 1732, was the last of Britain's thirteen

Ships at Jamestown, the first English colony.

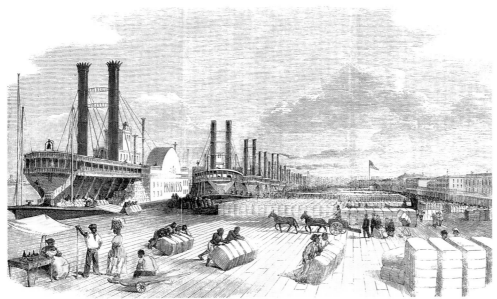

Mississippi riverboats at a port in New Orleans, Louisiana.

more and more on African slaves.

Traders brought the first Africans to Virginia in 1619. Like many new arrivals in the struggling colony, they were **indentured servants**. That is, after serving a period of years, the slaves could earn their freedom. That soon changed. By the 1660s, Africans were being bought and sold as slaves.

colonies to be settled. It became a refuge for English debtors and other former prisoners. Georgia also served as a buffer against the threat of Spanish invasion from Florida.

The English and Spanish were not the only Europeans in the region. In the 1600s, French explorers followed the Mississippi River into the South. Robert Cavalier reached the mouth of the river in 1682. He claimed the entire Mississippi valley for France. French colonies were founded in the region around 1700. France later gave the region to Spain.

Descendants of early French and Spanish settlers, called Creoles, still live in Louisiana. So do Cajuns, descendants of French Canadians who arrived in the area in the late 1700s.

EARLY DAYS

With plenty of good farmland and a mild climate, settlers in the South became successful farmers. They established huge plantations and grew highly profitable crops such as tobacco, rice, sugarcane, and cotton. Running these farms required a lot of labor. To fill the need, plantation owners came to rely

In 1775, patriots from Southern states were leaders in the fight for independence from Britain, which was called the Revolutionary War. The war's last major battle was fought at Yorktown, in Virginia. There, in 1781, British Lord Cornwallis surrendered to General George Washington. In the years after the war, Southern ports such as Charleston, South Carolina, grew into thriving cities. Settlers pushed across the mountains into Kentucky and the South Central region.

In 1803, the United States doubled its size with the Louisiana Purchase. This huge territory, acquired from France, included more than 800,000 square miles of land west of the Mississippi River. As settlers moved west, the river became the main transportation route to the U.S. heartland. New Orleans, at the mouth of the Mississippi, became one of the nation's busiest ports.

Think About It

How and why did Southerners come to depend on slavery?

Focus On: The Everglades

Southern Florida has one of North America's great natural wonders: the Everglades. Made up of swampy grasslands, scrub pine groves, and mangrove thickets, the Everglades covers 1.4 million acres. About a fifth of that area is protected in Everglades National Park. This subtropical wilderness is home to alligators, the rare Florida panther, and many kinds of birds.

In recent years, the Everglades have been harmed by pollution, water diversion, and other threats. Environmental groups and

Everglades National Park

government are working to correct these problems and protect the unique wildlife of the region.

By 1845, all the Southern states were part of the Union. The sole exception was West Virginia, which split from Virginia during the Civil War.

SOUTH AGAINST NORTH

During the 1800s, the South developed fewer industries than the Northeast. There were fewer immigrants, too. Farming remained the mainstay of Southern life, and Southern states continued to practice slavery, even as other states outlawed it. By 1860, there were roughly 4 million slaves in the South. They made up nearly a third of the population.

In the North, many people, called abolitionists, had come to see that slavery was

wrong. They wanted slavery to end. Southerners believed they needed slaves to work the plantations. Without slaves, they said, the South's economy would collapse.

In 1860 and 1861, slavery and other issues finally caused eleven southern states to secede, or leave the Union. The result was the Civil War, fought from 1861 to 1865.

Southern tobacco plantation, 1800s.

YOUNG EXPLORER

Can you find West Virginia on the map (page 24)?

Find the Mississippi River on the map. How did its location help make New Orleans a busy port city?

Freeing slaves in North Carolina, after 1865.

The North defeated the South, and the slaves were freed.

CHANGES IN THE SOUTH

The years after the Civil War saw great changes in the South. Without slaves, plantation owners sold their land or rented plots to tenant farmers, called **sharecroppers**. Farmers continued to rely on single cash crops, especially cotton. In the early 1900s, an insect called the boll weevil destroyed cotton crops throughout the region. This disaster taught farmers to grow a variety of crops.

Mining and manufacturing increased. West Virginia and Tennessee developed coal mines. Starting in the 1870s, New England textile companies began to build mills in the South. Before long, Southern factories were making textiles, clothing, furniture, paper, and other products.

In the early 1900s, oil refineries and chemical plants opened in Louisiana, to take advantage of Gulf Coast oil. In the 1930s, the Tennessee Valley Authority built a series of dams on the Tennessee River. The dams trapped water for irrigation and harnessed its power for electricity for the region.

These changes helped the South prosper, but life was still a struggle for former slaves and their descendants. Many Southern states practiced **segregation**. African Americans were separated from whites in everything from schools to restaurants. They were prevented from voting and denied good jobs. In the 1950s and 1960s, African Americans protested in what became known as the Civil Rights Movement.

Civil Rights march, 1963.

They finally won equal rights through court rulings. *Brown* versus *the Board of Education* in 1954 ruled that segregation in schools was unconstitutional, for example.

The same period saw new immigrants arriving in the South. Many Cubans left their homeland for Florida after a Communist government came to power there in the late 1950s. They settled in and around Miami.

Think About It

How has geography played a part in the South's history and growth?

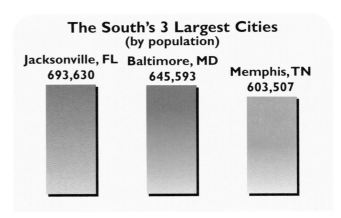

The South's 3 Largest Cities
(by population)

Jacksonville, FL	Baltimore, MD	Memphis, TN
693,630	645,593	603,507

Focus On: Washington, D.C.

Washington, D.C., the capital of the United States, is located between Virginia and Maryland, but it is not part of either state. In 1790, the U.S. Congress decided that the nation's capital should be in a federal district,

The Mall, Washington, D.C.

rather than in any state. The District of Columbia was named in honor of Christopher Columbus. The city itself was named in honor of George Washington, who picked the site on the Potomac River.

MAJOR CROPS AND INDUSTRIES OF THE SOUTH

WEST VIRGINIA
Major industries: Chemicals, iron and steel, glass and clay
Major farm products: Cattle, dairy products, apples, chickens

MARYLAND
Major industries: Electrical equipment, processed foods, printing
Major farm products: Poultry and eggs, dairy products, greenhouse and nursery products

DELAWARE
Major industries: Chemicals, processed foods, rubber and plastic products
Major farm products: Chickens, soybeans, corn, dairy products

TENNESSEE
Major industries: Chemicals and plastics, food products, motor vehicles
Major farm products: Cattle, hogs, dairy products, cotton

KENTUCKY
Major industries: Automobiles, textiles, electrical equipment
Major farm products: Tobacco, soybeans, corn, cattle

VIRGINIA
Major industries: Electronic equipment, machinery, processed foods, printing
Major farm products: Poultry, cattle, dairy products, tobacco

ARKANSAS
Major industries: Processed foods, electrical equipment, wood products
Major farm products: Chickens, soybeans, rice, wheat

NORTH CAROLINA
Major industries: Textiles, tobacco products, chemicals, wood and paper products
Major farm products: Tobacco, poultry, hogs, sweet potatoes

LOUISIANA
Major industries: Chemicals, petroleum, processed foods
Major farm products: Soybeans, cattle, rice, cotton

SOUTH CAROLINA
Major industries: Textiles, chemicals, machinery
Major farm products: Tobacco, soybeans, cattle, hogs

MISSISSIPPI
Major industries: Clothing, wood products, ships, tile and brick
Major farm products: Cotton, chickens, soybeans, cattle

ALABAMA
Major industries: Metals and metal products, paper and wood products, textiles
Major farm products: Chickens, cattle, hogs, dairy products

GEORGIA
Major industries: Textiles and clothing, transportation equipment, food products
Major farm products: Poultry and eggs, livestock, dairy products, peanuts

FLORIDA
Major industries: Electrical and electronic equipment, food products, printing
Major farm products: Citrus fruits, vegetables, greenhouse and nursery products

Dover
MD DE
★Annapolis
WV VA ★Richmond
★Charleston
Frankfort
KY
★Raleigh
NC
★Nashville
TN
SC ★Columbia
AR
Little Rock
★Atlanta
MS AL GA
Jackson ★Montgomery
LA
★Tallahassee
Baton Rouge
FL

Skyline in Atlanta, Georgia.

THE SOUTH TODAY

Farming is still important in the South. Today most farmers own, rather than rent, their farms. Among the South's leading products are soybeans, peanuts, and broiler chickens, as well as cotton and tobacco. Florida produces most of the oranges and other citrus fruits sold in the United States. Kentucky's horse farms are famous.

Mining and manufacturing are still important, too. New industries have come to the South as well. They have brought growth to many cities. Atlanta, Georgia, is a bustling business and financial center. Raleigh, North Carolina, is known for technology and scientific research. The aerospace industry is centered around the Kennedy Space Center at Cape Canaveral, Florida.

Florida remains a top tourist destination. It has more miles of beaches than any other state, plus many theme parks and attractions. People from many parts of the United States have chosen to retire in Florida and other southern states. Immigrants have come from Latin America, Asia, and other regions.

The new residents have helped bring greater variety to the South. Southerners old and new still honor the region's traditions of courtesy and hospitality.

CHAPTER REVIEW

1. What is the largest bay on the South's Atlantic coast?
2. What major southern river empties into the Gulf of Mexico?
3. What did Juan Ponce de Leon hope to find in Florida?
4. What cash crop helped save the Jamestown colony?
5. Louisiana's Creoles are descended from what groups?
6. How many slaves were in the South in 1860?
7. What insect destroyed cotton crops in the early 1900s?
8. What was the goal of the civil rights movement of the 1950s and 1960s?
9. Which state is famous for its horse farms?
10. Which state is a center of the aerospace industry?

Activities

Here is a list of some famous people who were born or lived in the South. Choose a person as a topic for a short report. Describe what your subject did and what was most important about his or her life. If possible, use the Internet for some of your research.

Alabama
HELEN KELLER, Educator
JESSE OWENS, Track star
ROSA PARKS, Civil rights leader

Arkansas
WILLIAM J. CLINTON, 42nd President of the United States
SCOTT JOPLIN, Musician and composer
DOUGLAS MACARTHUR, World War II general

Delaware
ANNIE JUMP CANNON, Astronomer
ELEUTHERE IRENEE DU PONT, Chemist
HOWARD PYLE, Author and artist

Florida
MARY MCLEOD BETHUNE, Educator
MARJORY STONEMAN DOUGLAS, Author
ZORA NEALE HURSTON, Author

Georgia
JAMES BOWIE, Frontiersman
JAMES EARL CARTER, JR., 39th President of the
    United States
MARTIN LUTHER KING, JR., Civil rights leader

Kentucky
MUHAMMAD ALI, Boxer
DANIEL BOONE, Frontiersman
CARRY NATION, Prohibitionist

Louisiana
LOUIS ARMSTRONG, Jazz musician
LILLIAN HELLMAN, Playwright
JEAN LAFFITE, Pirate

Maryland
GEORGE HERMAN (BABE) RUTH, Baseball star
FRANCES SCOTT KEY, Wrote "The Star-Spangled
    Banner"
THURGOOD MARSHALL, Supreme Court
    justice

Mississippi
JEFFERSON DAVIS, Confederate president
FANNIE LOU HAMER, Civil rights activist
ELVIS PRESLEY, Singer

North Carolina
MICHAEL JORDAN, Basketball star
DOLLEY MADISON, U.S. first lady
JAMES KNOX POLK, 11th President of the United
    States

South Carolina
SARAH and ANGELINA GRIMKE, Abolitionists
JESSE JACKSON, Civil rights leader and politician
FRANCIS MARION, Revolutionary War hero

Tennessee
DAVY CROCKETT, Frontiersman
ANDREW JACKSON, 7th President of the United
    States
WILMA RUDOLPH, Track star

Virginia
ELLA FITZGERALD, Singer
ROBERT E. LEE, Civil War general
GEORGE WASHINGTON, Revolutionary War hero
    and first U.S. president

West Virginia
PEARL S. BUCK, Author
THOMAS (STONEWALL) JACKSON, Civil War general
WALTER P. REUTHER, Labor leader

FOCUS ON: Celebrating the South

Here is a partial list of the many festivals and special events celebrated by towns and cities in the South. Choose one as the subject of a research paper. Then write about it in as much detail as possible, using the Internet to locate information.

ALABAMA
National Shrimp Festival
October, Gulf Shores

FLORIDA
Carnival Miami
February or March (week before Lent), Miami

LOUISIANA
Mardi Gras
February or March (before Lent), New Orleans

VIRGINIA
Jamestown Landing Day
May, Williamsburg

The Midwest

Between the Appalachians to the east and the Rocky Mountains to the west, fields and plains roll on for mile after mile. This is the Midwest, sometimes called the "heartland" of the United States. Good soil has made the Midwest the nation's richest farming region. The Great Lakes and major rivers have helped make it a center for industry and trade.

Twelve states make up the Midwest. They are sometimes divided into two groups. The East North Central states are Ohio, Michigan, Indiana, Illinois, and Wisconsin. The West North Central states are Minnesota, Iowa, Missouri, Kansas, Nebraska, North Dakota, and South Dakota.

CANADA

Lake Superior

0   500

ND
★ Bismark

SD
★ Pierre

BLACK HILLS

GREAT PLAINS

NE

Lincoln ★

Kansas City
Topeka ★

KS

Missouri R.

MN
CENTRAL
St. Paul ★   LOWLAND

WI
★ Madison

Mississippi R.

Des Moines R.

IA
★
Des Moines

Illinois R.

Jefferson City
★   • St. Louis

MO

OZARK PLATEAU

Lake Michigan

Lake Huron

MI
★   Detroit
Lansing   Lake Erie

Chicago   • Cleveland

IL   OH
★   Columbus
IN   ★
★   Ohio R.
Springfield   Indianapolis

Lake Ontario

N
W   E
S

THE LAND

Most of the Midwestern states are in a region called the Central Lowland. Its fertile plains run from the Canadian border south into Texas. To the west, in Kansas, Nebraska, and the Dakotas, the land rises to a high **plateau**. This is the Great Plains.

Iowa farmland

Badlands of South Dakota

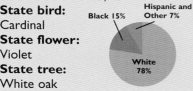

The Midwestern States

ILLINOIS

Area: 56,345 sq mi (145,935 km2)
Capital: Springfield
Statehood: December 3, 1818; the 21st state
Motto: "State sovereignty, national union"
Nickname: Land of Lincoln
Abbreviations: IL, Ill.
State bird: Cardinal
State flower: Violet
State tree: White oak

Black 15%
Hispanic and Other 7%
White 78%

INDIANA

Area: 36,185 sq mi (93,719 km2)
Capital: Indianapolis
Statehood: December 11, 1816; the 19th state
Motto: "The crossroads of America"
Nickname: Hoosier State
Abbreviations: IN, Ind.
State bird: Cardinal
State flower: Peony
State tree: Tulip tree

Black 8%
Hispanic and Other 1%
White 91%

IOWA

Area: 56,275 sq mi (145,752 km2)
Capital: Des Moines
Statehood: December 28, 1846; the 29th state
Motto: "Our liberties we prize and our rights we will maintain."
Nickname: Hawkeye State
Abbreviations: IA, Ia.
State bird: Eastern goldfinch
State flower: Wild rose
State tree: Oak

Black 2%
Hispanic and Other 1%
White 97%

KANSAS

Area: 82,277 sq mi (213,098 km2)
Capital: Topeka
Statehood: January 29, 1861; the 34th state
Motto: *Ad astra per aspera* (To the stars through difficulties).
Nickname: Sunflower State
Abbreviations: KS, Kan.
State bird: Western meadowlark
State flower: Sunflower
State tree: Cottonwood

Black 6%
Hispanic and Other 4%
White 90%

MICHIGAN

Area: 58,527 sq mi (151,586 km2)
Capital: Lansing
Statehood: January 26, 1837; the 26th state
Motto: *Si quaeris peninsulam amoenam circumspice* (If you seek a pleasant peninsula, look around you).
Nickname: Wolverine State
Abbreviations: MI, Mich.
State bird: Robin
State flower: Apple blossom
State tree: White pine

Black 14%
Hispanic and Other 2%
White 84%

MINNESOTA

Area: 84,402 sq mi (218,601 km2)
Capital: St. Paul
Statehood: May 11, 1868; the 32nd state
Motto: *L'Etoile du Nord* (Star of the North).
Nickname: North Star State
Abbreviations: MN, Minn.
State bird: Common loon
State flower: Showy lady's slipper
State tree: Red (Norway) pine

Black, Asian, and Hispanic 6%
White 94%

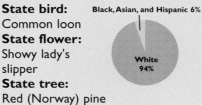

MISSOURI

Area: 69,697 sq mi (180,516 km2)
Capital: Jefferson City
Statehood: August 10, 1821; the 24th state
Motto: *Salus populi suprema lex esto* (The welfare of the people shall be the supreme law).
Nickname: Show Me State
Abbreviations: MO, Mo.
State bird: Eastern bluebird
State flower: Hawthorn
State tree: Dogwood

Black 11%
Hispanic and Other 1%
White 88%

NEBRASKA

Area: 77,355 sq mi (200,350 km2)
Capital: Lincoln
Statehood: March 1, 1867; the 37th state
Motto: "Equality before the law"
Nickname: Cornhusker State
Abbreviations: NE; Neb.
State bird: Western meadowlark
State flower: Goldenrod
State tree: Cottonwood

Black 4%
Hispanic and Other 2%
White 94%

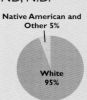

NORTH DAKOTA

Area: 70,702 sq mi (183,119 km2)
Capital: Bismark
Statehood: November 2, 1889; the 39th state
Motto: "Liberty and union, now and forever: one and inseparable"
Nickname: Flickertail State
Abbreviations: ND, N.D.
State bird: Western meadowlark
State flower: Prairie rose
State tree: American elm

Native American and Other 5%
White 95%

OHIO

Area: 40,953 sq mi. (106,067 km2)
Capital: Columbus
Statehood: March 1, 1803;
the 17th state
State motto: "With God, all
things are possible."
Nickname: Buckeye State
Abbreviations: OH, Oh.
State bird:
Cardinal
State flower:
Scarlet carnation
State tree:
Buckeye

Black 11%
Hispanic and Other 1%
White 88%

SOUTH DAKOTA

Area: 77,116 sq mi (199730 km2)
Capital: Pierre
Statehood: November 2, 1889;
the 40th state
Motto: "Under God the people
rule."
Nickname: Mount Rushmore State
Abbreviations: SD, S.D.
State bird:
Ring-necked
pheasant
State flower:
Pasqueflower
State tree:
Black Hills
spruce

Native American 7%
Black and Hispanic 1%
White 92%

WISCONSIN

Area: 56,153 sq mi (145,436 km2)
Capital: Madison
Statehood: May 29, 1848;
the 30th state
Motto: "Forward"
Nickname: Badger State
Abbreviations: WI, Wis.
State bird:
Robin
State flower:
Violet
State tree:
Sugar maple

Black 5%
Hispanic and Other 2%
White 93%

In many parts of the Midwest, flat land stretches away as far as the eye can see. The flat plains remind some visitors of the surface of the ocean. The Midwest is not all level. In Ohio, the land drops down from the Appalachians through rolling hills. Southern Missouri has the uplands of the Ozark Plateau. The Great Plains are broken in some areas by sandhills and strangely eroded **badlands**. The Black Hills, a group of mountains, rise abruptly from the plains in South Dakota.

The five Great Lakes lie along the border between the United States and Canada. The lakes— Ontario, Erie, Huron, Michigan, and Superior—are all connected. They stretch about 850 miles east to west and 700 miles north to south. Together, they form the largest body of fresh water in the world. In the country's early days, the Great Lakes provided a water route into the Midwest. They are still important to the region.

Rivers have also played an important part in the Midwest's growth. The Mississippi River begins in northern Minnesota and flows south to the Gulf of Mexico. Hundreds of other rivers flow into it. Among the largest are the Missouri and Ohio. The Missouri, the second-longest river in the United States, joins the Mississippi (the longest river) from the west near Alton, Illinois. The Ohio enters from the east near Cairo, Illinois.

Hot summers and cold winters are usual in the Midwest. The northern plains and the Great Lakes regions see deep winter snows and bitter temperatures. Spring brings mild, pleasant days. Melting snows and spring rains often cause Midwestern rivers to flood.

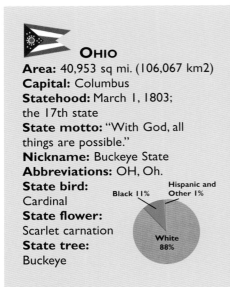

Mississippi River

Severe thunderstorms and tornadoes are common. On average, the Great Plains get less rain than the Central Lowland. From time to time, drought strikes the Midwest, bringing disaster to farmers and ranchers.

Originally, forests covered much of this land. From Illinois west, there were **prairies** with grass that stood taller than a person. Now corn, soybeans, and other crops are grown in the Central Lowland. Ranches and huge wheat farms spread over the Great Plains. There are still some forests. The largest ones are in northern Minnesota, southern Missouri, and the Black Hills. Sections of tallgrass prairie remain in Minnesota and a few other areas.

The grasslands of the Midwest were once home to vast herds of bison. Now most of the bison are gone, along with the grasslands. The Midwest still has wild animals, including deer, coyotes, and many smaller creatures. Timber wolves, black bears, and moose roam the Minnesota woods. Gophers and prairie dogs live on the plains.

This region's rich soil is its greatest natural resource. Copper, iron, and other ores are mined in the Great Lakes region. One of the biggest gold mines in the United States is in the Black Hills of South Dakota.

Bison herd at Custer State Park, in South Dakota.

YOUNG EXPLORER

Can you find the Great Lakes on the map (page 34)?

Why do you think the Great Lakes were so important to the Midwest's growth?

EUROPEANS ARRIVE

French explorers were the first Europeans in the Midwest. Jacques Cartier explored the St. Lawrence River, which leads to the Great Lakes, in 1534 and 1535. Samuel de Champlain reached Lake Ontario and Lake Huron in 1615. Father Jacques Marquette and Louis Jolliet sailed down the Mississippi River in 1673. French fur traders and **missionaries** continued exploring the region, which they claimed as New France. The French founded Detroit in 1701. Other settlements followed.

Britain took control of what had been New France in the 1760s. After the Revolutionary War in 1781, the United States gained control of the region between the Appalachians and the Mississippi. American fur traders and settlers soon began to move into the Northwest Territory, as this region was then called. They cleared land for farming and built log homes.

The United States obtained most of the rest of what is today the Midwest as part of the Louisiana Purchase, in 1803. Before long, settlers were flocking to Missouri and other areas west of the Mississippi.

EARLY DAYS

Rivers were the highways of the newly settled lands, carrying people and goods. The Great Lakes also played a major role in the growth of settlements. The lakes became especially important after the Erie Canal opened in 1825. The canal linked the lakes to the

Focus On: The Black Hills

The Black Hills are a group of ancient mountains that rise sharply from the Great Plains in South Dakota. The mountains were held sacred by the Sioux Indians of this region. Among the forested peaks are many strange formations. They include the Needles, a group of towering granite spikes, and Wind Cave, a 40-mile network of underground caverns. Mount Rushmore, carved in granite with the images of four U.S. presidents, is in the Black Hills.

Mount Rushmore

Hudson River, allowing goods to be shipped by barge to New York City.

Towns and cities sprang up on the lakes and rivers. Cleveland, Detroit, and Chicago developed into important Great Lakes ports. River ports included St. Louis, on the Mississippi; and Kansas City, on the Missouri. These cities became starting points for wagon trains that took pioneers west, to Oregon and California.

One by one, as their populations grew, Midwestern territories joined the Union as states. Several territories were caught up in the debate over slavery that led up to the

Riverboat on the Mississippi River.

Civil War. Northerners wanted slavery to be outlawed in new states. Southerners wanted slavery to be permitted. Missouri's statehood was delayed by the issue. In a compromise, Missouri finally entered the Union in 1821 as a slave state, along with Maine, a free state. In the 1850s, the slavery issue led to violence in Kansas and Nebraska.

THE MIDWEST GROWS

After the Civil War (1861–1865), new waves of settlers arrived. They were encouraged by the Homestead Act, which had been passed in 1862. It offered 160 acres of free land to anyone who would farm and live on it. New railroads made it easier to travel and ship

In 1860, Lincoln and Hamlin ran on a platform to end slavery.

Pioneers of the West.

Lake Michigan, one of the five Great Lakes.

goods, too. Among the new settlers were people from Scandinavia, Germany, Ireland, Poland, and other European countries.

Homesteaders soon began to plow the Great Plains. With no lumber available, these "sodbusters" built their first homes of sod blocks made from grass-covered earth. Life on the plains was hard. With windmills to pump water from below ground, barbed wire for fencing, and machines for large-scale farming, they succeeded.

Settlement brought an end to the Plains Indians' traditional way of life. The Plains groups were defeated in a series of wars. The bison herds they depended on were wiped out by overhunting. Farms and towns began to spread across the land that had once "belonged" to the Indians. By the 1880s, most of them had been pushed onto **reservations**.

By that time, too, industry was growing in the Midwest. Chicago, Kansas City, and other

 FOCUS ON: **Chicago's Great Fire**

In October 1871, fire swept through the city of Chicago. A legend says that a cow owned by a Mrs. O'Leary kicked over a lantern and started the fire. That's just a story. No one knows how the fire began.

However the fire started, nearly 18,000 wooden buildings burned down. Chicagoans rebuilt their city in just two years. This time, they used materials that wouldn't burn—brick, stone, cast iron, and steel.

Downtown Chicago

cities became centers for meatpacking, food processing, and other farm-related industries. Mining and manufacturing increased, too. In the early 1900s, Detroit became the center of the new automobile industry.

These growing industries needed workers. That need brought people from the East and from various parts of Europe to the Midwest. In the late 1800s and early 1900s, many African Americans arrived from the South, looking for greater opportunities.

Growth brought problems as well as prosperity, however. Mining and manufacturing created serious pollution, especially around the Great Lakes. In the 1930s, a severe drought struck the Great Plains and Southwest. Without grass to hold it in place, the plowed soil of the plains turned to dust. Huge, dusty clouds were carried off by the wind. The region became known as the Dust Bowl. Better farming methods have since helped to prevent similar disasters.

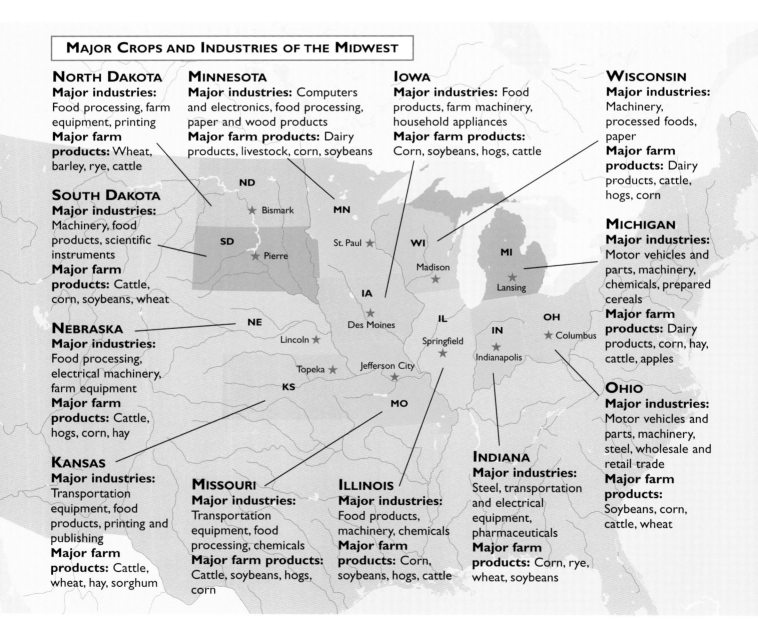

MAJOR CROPS AND INDUSTRIES OF THE MIDWEST

NORTH DAKOTA
Major industries: Food processing, farm equipment, printing
Major farm products: Wheat, barley, rye, cattle

SOUTH DAKOTA
Major industries: Machinery, food products, scientific instruments
Major farm products: Cattle, corn, soybeans, wheat

NEBRASKA
Major industries: Food processing, electrical machinery, farm equipment
Major farm products: Cattle, hogs, corn, hay

KANSAS
Major industries: Transportation equipment, food products, printing and publishing
Major farm products: Cattle, wheat, hay, sorghum

MINNESOTA
Major industries: Computers and electronics, food processing, paper and wood products
Major farm products: Dairy products, livestock, corn, soybeans

MISSOURI
Major industries: Transportation equipment, food processing, chemicals
Major farm products: Cattle, soybeans, hogs, corn

IOWA
Major industries: Food products, farm machinery, household appliances
Major farm products: Corn, soybeans, hogs, cattle

ILLINOIS
Major industries: Food products, machinery, chemicals
Major farm products: Corn, soybeans, hogs, cattle

INDIANA
Major industries: Steel, transportation and electrical equipment, pharmaceuticals
Major farm products: Corn, rye, wheat, soybeans

WISCONSIN
Major industries: Machinery, processed foods, paper
Major farm products: Dairy products, cattle, hogs, corn

MICHIGAN
Major industries: Motor vehicles and parts, machinery, chemicals, prepared cereals
Major farm products: Dairy products, corn, hay, cattle, apples

OHIO
Major industries: Motor vehicles and parts, machinery, steel, wholesale and retail trade
Major farm products: Soybeans, corn, cattle, wheat

ND
Bismark ★
SD
★ Pierre
MN
St. Paul ★
WI
Madison ★
MI
★ Lansing
IA
★ Des Moines
NE
Lincoln ★
IL
Springfield ★
IN
★ Indianapolis
OH
★ Columbus
Topeka ★
Jefferson City ★
KS
MO

Think About It

Why did so many settlers migrate to the Midwest? What made it appealing?

THE MIDWEST TODAY

Since the 1960s, manufacturing has declined in the Midwest. Many companies have moved their factories south or overseas, to places where the cost of doing business is less. That has put many people out of work. However, the Midwest is still one of the most important regions in North America for industry, farming, and trade. Many cities have worked hard to bring in new industries. Chicago is the region's biggest commercial center. From its port, ships reach the Atlantic Ocean, by way of the St. Lawrence Seaway, and the Gulf of Mexico, by way of the Illinois and Mississippi rivers.

Like cities elsewhere in the United States, Midwestern cities are ringed by suburbs. Beyond the suburbs, farms still stretch for miles. Many modern farms and ranches are huge, covering thousands of acres. They are true businesses, using big machines in the fields and computers to keep track of operations.

Midwestern states have also made strides in cleaning up pollution. From the northern

The Gateway Arch welcomes visitors to St. Louis, Missouri.

Minnesota lakes to the Ozarks, vacationers enjoy fishing, boating, and camping in state and national parks. They also come to see attractions such as the Gateway Arch in St. Louis. This soaring arch stands on the shore of the Mississippi River as a monument to the pioneers who helped to build the region.

Detroit skyline

The Midwest's 3 Largest Cities
(by population)

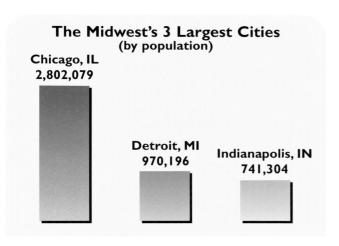

Chicago, IL
2,802,079

Detroit, MI
970,196

Indianapolis, IN
741,304

CHAPTER REVIEW

1. Where are the Great Plains?
2. Name the five Great Lakes.
3. What is the longest river in the United States?
4. From what country did the first Europeans in the Midwest come?
5. What was the Northwest Territory?
6. In what territories did the issue of slavery lead to violence?
7. How much free land could settlers get under the Homestead Act of 1862?
8. Where is Mount Rushmore?
9. What Midwestern city became the center of the automobile industry?
10. What city is the Midwest's largest commercial center today?

Activities

Here is a list of some famous people who were born or lived in the Midwest. Choose a person as a topic for a short report. Describe what your subject did and what was most important about his or her life. If possible, use the Internet for some of your research.

Illinois
JANE ADDAMS, Social worker
WALT DISNEY, Cartoonist
CARL SANDBURG, Poet

Indiana
EUGENE DEBS, Labor leader
WILLIAM HENRY HARRISON, U.S. president
JESSAMYN WEST, Writer

View of Minneapolis, Minnesota. Its "twin city," across the Mississippi River, is St. Paul.

Iowa
WILLIAM (BUFFALO BILL) CODY, Frontiersman
HERBERT HOOVER, U.S. president
GRANT WOOD, Artist

Kansas
AMELIA EARHART, Aviator
DWIGHT D. EISENHOWER, U.S. president
CHARLIE PARKER, Jazz musician

Michigan
GERALD FORD, U.S. President
WILL KEITH KELLOGG, Cereal maker
SUGAR RAY ROBINSON, Boxer

Minnesota
JUDY GARLAND, Actress and singer
J. PAUL GETTY, Businessman
CHARLES M. SCHULZ, Cartoonist

Missouri
HARRY S. TRUMAN, U.S. president
MARK TWAIN (SAMUEL CLEMENS), Writer
GEORGE WASHINGTON CARVER, Agricultural chemist

Nebraska
WILLIAM JENNINGS BRYAN, Political leader
WILLA CATHER, Writer
CRAZY HORSE (TASHUNCA-UITCO), Sioux leader

North Dakota
PEGGY LEE, Jazz singer
MANUEL LISA, Fur trader
LAWRENCE WELK, Entertainer

Ohio
NEIL ARMSTRONG, Astronaut
ANNIE OAKLEY, Markswoman
ORVILLE WRIGHT, Inventor

South Dakota
GERTRUDE SIMMONS BONNIN, Writer
SITTING BULL (TATANKA LYOTAKE), Sioux leader
GEORGE S. MCGOVERN, Politician

Wisconsin
ROY CHAPMAN ANDREWS, Scientist and explorer
CARRIE CHAPMAN CATT, Women's rights leader
LAURA INGALLS WILDER, Writer

 FOCUS ON: **Celebrating the Midwest**

Here is a partial list of the many festivals celebrated by towns and cities across the Midwest. Choose one as the subject for a research paper. Then write about it as in as much detail as possible. Use the Internet for some of your research.

ILLINOIS
International Livestock Exposition
November, Chicago

INDIANA
Indianapolis 500 Race
Saturday before Memorial Day, Indianapolis

KANSAS
Santa Fe Trail Days
May, Larned

MISSOURI
Tom Sawyer Days
July, Hannibal

NEBRASKA
Nebraskaland Days
June, North Platte

OHIO
Cityfolk Festival
June, Dayton

SOUTH DAKOTA
Laura Ingalls Wilder Pageant
July, De Smet

WISCONSIN
Great Wisconsin Cheese Festival
June, Little Chute

The Mountain States

In 1869, the explorer John Wesley Powell looked down over the meeting of the Colorado River and the Green River in Utah. "What a world of grandeur is spread before us!" he exclaimed. Most visitors to the mountain states would agree.

The rivers that Powell saw rush down out of the Rocky Mountains. This spectacular mountain chain has been called the "backbone" of North America. The Rockies stretch all the way from northern Alaska to Colorado and northern New Mexico. They include some of the tallest peaks in the United States. For pioneers headed west, the mountains were a challenging barrier. Today, people come to the Rockies from all over the world, for a glimpse of the dramatic wilderness that Powell first saw.

John Wesley Powell

Five states straddle the Rockies. They are Montana, Wyoming, Idaho, Colorado, and Utah. Nevada, in the high desert, west of the Rockies, completes the Mountain States group.

THE LAND

The eastern parts of three mountain states—Montana, Wyoming, and Colorado—lie on the Great Plains. This part of the prairie is sometimes called the High Plains, because the land is higher here than in the eastern Plains. From the High Plains, the mountains rise like a great wall. Their snow-covered peaks can be seen from miles away.

The Rocky Mountains are the most important mountain chain in the United

Rocky Mountains, Colorado

 **AT A GLANCE**

The Mountain States

 COLORADO

Area: 104,091 sq mi (269,595 km2)
Capital: Denver
Statehood: August 1, 1876; the 38th state
Motto: *Nil sine numine* (Nothing without providence).
Nickname: Centennial State
Abbreviations: CO, Colo.
State bird: Lark bunting
State flower: Rocky Mountain columbine
State tree: Colorado blue spruce

Black 3%
Hispanic and Other 11%
White 86%

 IDAHO

Area: 83,564 sq mi (216,432 km2)
Capital: Boise
Statehood: July 3, 1890; the 43rd state
Motto: *Esto perpetua* (May it last forever).
Nickname: Gem State
Abbreviations: ID, Ida.
State bird: Mountain bluebird
State flower: Syringa (mock orange)
State tree: Western white pine

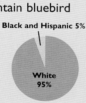
Black and Hispanic 5%
White 95%

 MONTANA

Area: 147,046 sq mi (380,848 km2)
Capital: Helena
Statehood: November 8, 1889; the 41st state
Motto: *Oro y plata* (Gold and silver).
Nickname: Treasure State
Abbreviations: MT, Mont.
State bird: Western meadowlark
State flower: Bitterroot
State tree: Ponderosa pine

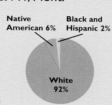
Native American 6%
Black and Hispanic 2%
White 92%

 NEVADA

Area: 110,561 sq mi (286,352 km2)
Capital: Carson City
Statehood: October 31, 1864; the 36th state
Motto: "All for our country"
Nickname: Silver State
Abbreviations: NV, Nev.
State bird: Mountain bluebird
State flower: Sagebrush
State tree: Single-leaf pinon

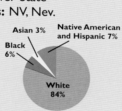
Asian 3%
Black 6%
Native American and Hispanic 7%
White 84%

 UTAH

Area: 84,899 sq mi (219,888 km2)
Capital: Salt Lake City
Statehood: January 4, 1896; the 45th state
Motto: "Industry"
Nickname: Beehive State
Abbreviation: UT
State bird: California gull
State flower: Sego lily
State tree: Blue spruce

Black 1%
Hispanic and Other 5%
White 94%

 WYOMING

Area: 97,809 sq mi (253,326 km2)
Capital: Cheyenne
Statehood: July 10, 1890; the 44th state
Motto: "Equal rights"
Nickname: Equality State
Abbreviations: WY, Wyo.
State bird: Western meadowlark
State flower: Indian paintbrush
State tree: Cottonwood

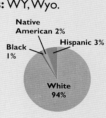
Native American 2%
Black 1%
Hispanic 3%
White 94%

States. In the lower 48 states, they are divided into three groups. The Northern Rockies rise in western Montana and Idaho. They include the Bitterroot and Clearwater ranges. The Middle Rockies lie mainly in Wyoming. They include the Bighorn range. South of the Middle Rockies is a high plateau, the Wyoming Basin. It's actually an extension of the Great Plains. The Oregon Trail, which took many pioneers west, passed through this plateau.

The Southern Rockies are mainly in Colorado. They include the chain's highest peak, Mt. Elbert, at 14,433 feet. Overall, the Rockies are more than twice as high as the

 YOUNG EXPLORER

Can you find the place on the map (page 44) where John Wesley Powell made his famous comment?

Lake Powell, Utah

Appalachians. Even the lowest passes through the Rockies are higher than most Appalachian peaks.

West of the Rockies' peaks, the land drops off to high plateaus. In some places, rivers have cut deep canyons and gorges. Nearly all of Nevada and much of Utah lie in a region called the Great Basin. This is a rugged land, with isolated mountains and dry valleys.

The Rocky Mountains are the site of the Continental Divide. The divide is an imaginary line that runs north to south through the heart of the mountain chain. East of the line, streams flow toward the Gulf of Mexico. West of the line, streams flow toward the Pacific.

Some of the streams flow on to become major rivers. The Missouri River begins in Montana and flows east and south to meet the Mississippi River. The Colorado River begins in Colorado and flows southwest to the Gulf of California. In the western deserts, many streams never reach the sea. They empty into salty lakes, such as Great Salt Lake in Utah, or simply peter out.

Hot summers and cold winters are the rule for the deserts and other lowland regions. Because of their great height, the mountains have a cool climate year-round. In the north, winters can bring temperatures of -40 degrees Fahrenheit.

The mountains also get more rain and snow than lower areas. Nevada is the driest of the 50 states, with less rain and snow than any other. The mountains lift westerly winds. As the rising air cools, it releases

Focus On: Yellowstone National Park

Jets of water and steam shoot into the sky. Mud holes and strangely colored hot springs dot the land. Those are some of the odd features at Yellowstone National Park. Founded in 1872, Yellowstone is the oldest national park in the world. It is also home to one of the highest waterfalls in the United States. The park is mostly in northwestern Wyoming. Besides **geysers** and hot springs, it preserves 3,462 square miles of Rocky Mountain wilderness. Among the many wild animals that live here are endangered bison and grizzly bears.

Old Faithful (above) and Yellowstone Falls (right).

Marker on the Continental Divide in Wyoming.

moisture. Rain and snow in the mountains feed rivers and lakes. This provides water for farming and for cities such as Denver, Colorado, and Salt Lake City, Utah.

The high Rocky Mountain peaks are bare, but thick forests cover most of the lower slopes. Ponderosa pine and other forest trees are an important source of lumber. The Rocky Mountains are also rich in minerals. Miners have found gold, silver, copper, lead, and zinc. Uranium, petroleum, and coal can also be found, especially in the region west of the mountains.

The mountain states are home to a wide range of wildlife—mule deer, elk, pronghorn, mountain lions, bobcats, black bears, coyotes, and many smaller animals. Gray wolves were once common. They were hunted until they disappeared from the region. Now some wolves have been brought back in some wilderness regions.

EARLY DAYS

The Spanish were the first Europeans to visit the mountain region. The explorer Francisco Coronado led an **expedition** into the Southern Rockies in the 1540s. Indians were the only people living in the region until well into the 1800s.

On their 1804-06 expedition to explore the Louisiana Purchase, Meriwether Lewis and William Clark crossed the rugged Northern Rockies. They were the first explorers to do so. Lewis and Clark explored other routes on the way home. They brought back word that the mountains teamed with beavers, valued for their furs. Soon, fur traders and trappers were pouring into the mountain area.

Trappers and traders—mountain men—found the best routes through the Rockies. As settlers headed from Eastern states to Oregon and California, mountain men guided them. From 1839 on, some 300,000 people crossed by way of the Oregon Trail. It followed the course of the North Platte and Sweetwater rivers to South Pass, in Wyoming. East of Great Salt Lake, the trail split. Southern branches led across the desert toward California. The main trail continued on to Oregon.

 Think About It

How did the explorers find the best routes through the mountains? What characteristics would the best routes have?

Lewis and Clark explored the Rockies in the 1800s and met Native Americans for the first time.

Salt Lake City, Utah (above), and Joseph Smith (inset).

MINERS AND SETTLERS

Most settlers followed the trails all the way to the West Coast. They wanted to cross the mountains—not stay there. Among the first to put down roots in the mountain states were the Mormons, members of the Church of Jesus Christ of Latter-Day Saints. Led by Joseph Smith, they founded Salt Lake City in 1847.

More people arrived in the 1850s, when gold and silver were found in the Rockies. While miners staked claims in the mountains, farmers and ranchers staked claims in the foothills. Indians who had long called the region home were pushed onto reservations.

In 1869, the first **transcontinental railroad** line was completed at Promontory, Utah. New railroads made the mountains easier to cross, and more people came. Mining camps and watering stops grew into towns—Denver, Cheyenne, Virginia City, and others. These "**boomtowns**" were rough places, where disputes were settled by gunfights. Most often wild west towns like these helped to create the legends of the Old West.

YOUNG EXPLORER

Can you find Utah on the map (page 44)?

Why do you think Utah was chosen as the place to complete the transcontinental railroad?

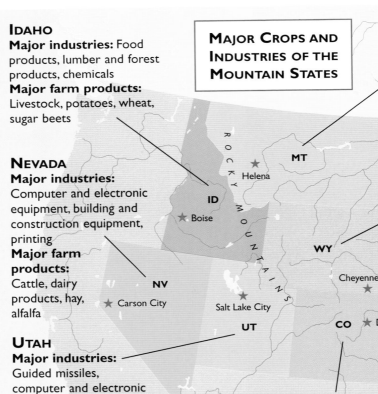

MAJOR CROPS AND INDUSTRIES OF THE MOUNTAIN STATES

IDAHO
Major industries: Food products, lumber and forest products, chemicals
Major farm products: Livestock, potatoes, wheat, sugar beets

NEVADA
Major industries: Computer and electronic equipment, building and construction equipment, printing
Major farm products: Cattle, dairy products, hay, alfalfa

UTAH
Major industries: Guided missiles, computer and electronic equipment, food products, metal products
Major farm products: Cattle, dairy products, hay, turkeys

MONTANA
Major industries: Lumber and wood products, petroleum and coal products, food products
Major farm products: Cattle, wheat, barley, hay

WYOMING
Major industries: Petroleum, food products, wood products
Major farm products: Cattle, sheep, sugar beets, hay

COLORADO
Major industries: Machinery, processed foods, computer and electronic equipment
Major farm products: Cattle, corn, wheat, dairy products

MT
Helena
ID
Boise
NV
Carson City
Salt Lake City
UT
WY
Cheyenne
CO
Denver
ROCKY MOUNTAINS

FOCUS ON: Hoover Dam

Hoover Dam blocks the Colorado River southeast of Las Vegas, Nevada. Standing 726 feet tall, it is one of the largest concrete dams in the world. The dam was completed in 1936, and it is still considered a major engineering achievement. A power plant in the base of the dam produces electricity. Behind the dam, the waters of the Colorado form Lake Mead. This lake, which lies between Nevada and Arizona, is the largest humanmade lake in the United States.

Hoover Dam

One by one, as their populations grew, the mountain states joined the Union. Nevada was the first to join, in 1864. Utah was the last, in 1896.

THE MOUNTAIN STATES TODAY

The mountain states grew dramatically in the 20th century. Beginning in the 1930s, some of the country's biggest dams were built in the area. The dams created a steady water supply. They also produced **hydroelectric power**. With water and electricity, growth took off.

Today, Denver is the biggest city on the eastern slopes of the Rockies. It's a business and cultural center for the entire region. Denver has several colleges and universities, an international airport, and major sports teams. Salt Lake City is the major center on the plateaus west of the Rockies. It is still best known as the home of the Mormon church. Farther west, Las Vegas, Nevada, lights up the desert sky at night with its neon signs. Las Vegas is famous for its gambling casinos, nightclubs, and hotels. It's also one of the fastest growing cities in the nation.

Many of the old Rocky Mountain mining camps are ghost towns today. They were abandoned when the gold or silver ran out. Mining, however, is still important in the mountain states.

Denver is called the "Mile High City" because the state capital is on land one mile above sea level.

Nightlife in Las Vegas, Nevada.

So are logging and ranching. Tourism is important. The mountain states are famous for their dramatic scenery, ski resorts, and national parks and forests. The federal government owns millions of acres in these states.

Growth in the mountain states has brought some problems. Air pollution troubles Denver and other cities. Ranchers and developers compete for scarce water resources. Many people worry that development, mining, logging, and tourism will damage the remaining wilderness. They hope to see at least some of this region stay as wild as it was when Lewis and Clark passed through.

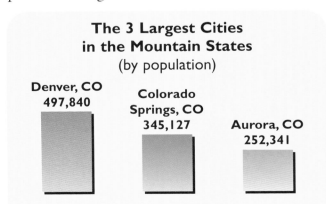

**The 3 Largest Cities
in the Mountain States**
(by population)

Denver, CO
497,840

Colorado
Springs, CO
345,127

Aurora, CO
252,341

Waterfall at Mt. Clement, Montana.

CHAPTER REVIEW

1. In what states are the Northern Rockies?
2. What is the highest peak in the Rockies?
3. What is the Continental Divide?
4. Which mountain state is the driest in the nation?
5. When did the Lewis and Clark expedition cross the Rockies?
6. Where did the Mormons settle?
7. When was the first transcontinental railroad line completed?
8. What is the largest city on the eastern slopes of the Rockies?
9. What city is famous for its casinos and hotels?
10. Name one problem that growth has brought to the mountain states.

FOCUS ON: Celebrating the Mountain States

Here is a partial list of the many festivals and special events celebrated by towns and cities in the Mountain States. Choose one as the subject of a research paper. Then write about it in as much detail as possible. Use the Internet to locate research material.

COLORADO
Pikes Peak or Bust Rodeo
August, Colorado Springs

IDAHO
Yellow Pine Harmonica Fest
August, Yellow Pine

MONTANA
Last Chance Fair and Stampede
July, Helena

NEVADA
Mule Show and Races
June, Winnemucca

UTAH
Days of '47 Celebration
July, Salt Lake City

WYOMING
Plains Indian Powwow
June, Cody

Activities

Here is a list of some famous people who were born or lived in the Mountain States. Choose a person as a topic for a short report. Describe what your subject did and what was most important about his or her life. If possible, use Internet sites for some of your research.

Colorado
SCOTT CARPENTER, Astronaut
JACK DEMPSEY, Boxer
SCOTT HAMILTON, Ice skater
HENRY A.W. TABOR, Mining magnate and U.S. senator

Idaho
TAFT BENSON, Politician
GUTZON BORGLUM, Sculptor
ERNEST HEMINGWAY, Writer
CHIEF JOSEPH, Nez Percé chief
SACAGAWEA, Shoshoni scout

Montana
CALAMITY JANE (MARTHA JANE CANARY), Sharpshooter
GARY COOPER, Actor
MARCUS DALY, Mining magnate

Nevada
ANDRE AGASSI, Tennis player
SARAH WINNEMUCCA HOPKINS, Native rights advocate
HOWARD HUGHES, Businessman
WOVOKA, Paiute prophet

Utah
MAUDE ADAMS, Actress
JOHN MOSES BROWNING, Inventor
EMMELINE B. WELLS, Women's rights advocate
BRIGHAM YOUNG, Religious and political leader

Wyoming
JAMES BRIDGER, Fur trapper and explorer
NELLIE TAYLOE ROSS, State governor and U.S. Mint director
J.C. PENNEY, Businessman
JACKSON POLLOCK, Artist

The Southwest

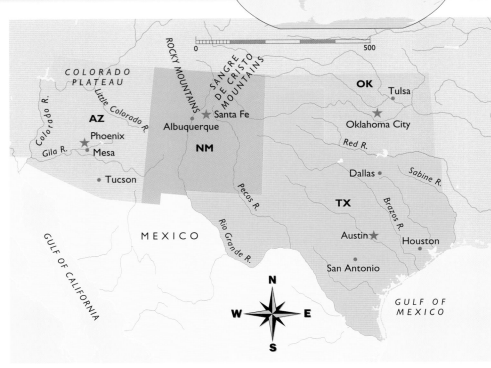

Deserts, mountains, and wide open spaces—the Southwest is famous for its landscapes. This region runs from the Gulf of Mexico north into the Great Plains. It reaches west across the southern tip of the Rocky Mountains to the Colorado River, which has carved deep canyons in the land.

Native Americans and Mexicans were at home here long before English-speaking settlers arrived. The Southwest was also part of the legendary Old West, with its cattle ranches and cowboys. Today, it is a thriving place, with a way of life as varied and lively as its history and scenery.

Just four states make up the Southwest— Texas, Oklahoma, New Mexico, and Arizona. Together, these four states make up a sixth of the total land area of the United States.

Mission in Albuquerque, New Mexico.

THE LAND
The Southwest has almost every kind of landscape. A coastal plain runs along the Gulf of Mexico through Texas. Here, forests of pine and cypress stand amid low-lying fields where rice is grown. Inland, the land rises to rolling hills with stands of oak and hickory. The hills give way to high plains, with grasslands and thickets of mesquite and sagebrush. The high plains cover most of Texas and western Oklahoma.

Organ pipe cacti fill the Arizona desert.

AT A GLANCE

The Southwest States

ARIZONA
Area: 114,000 sq mi (295,260 km2)
Capital: Phoenix
Statehood: February 14,, 1912; the 48th state
Motto: *Ditat Deus* (God enriches).
Nickname: Grand Canyon State
Abbreviations: AZ, Ariz.
State bird: Cactus wren
State flower: Saguaro cactus blossom
State tree: Paloverde

Native American 6% · Hispanic and Other 11% · White 80% · Black 3%

NEW MEXICO
Area: 121,593 sq mi (314,925 km2)
Capital: Santa Fe
Statehood: January 6, 1912; the 47th state
Motto: *Crescit Eundo* (It grows as it goes).
Nickname: Land of Enchantment
Abbreviations: NM, N. Mex.
State bird: Roadrunner
State flower: Yucca
State tree: Pinon

Native American 9% · Black 2% · White 49% · Hispanic and Other 40%

OKLAHOMA
Area: 69,956 sq mi (181,186 km2)
Capital: Oklahoma City
Statehood: November 16, 1907; the 46th state
Motto: *Labor omnia vincit* (Labor conquers all).
Nickname: Sooner State
Abbreviations: OK, Okla.
State bird: Scissor-tailed flycatcher
State flower: Mistletoe
State tree: Redbud

Native American 8% · Hispanic and Other 3% · White 82% · Black 7%

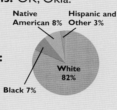

TEXAS
Area: 266,807 sq mi (691,030 km2)
Capital: Austin
Statehood: December 29, 1845; the 28th state
Motto: "Friendship"
Nickname: Lone Star State
Abbreviations: TX, Tex.
State bird: Mockingbird
State flower: Bluebonnet
State tree: Pecan

Hispanic and Other 26% · Black 11% · White 63%

They extend as far west as the Pecos River in New Mexico.

The Sangre de Cristo Mountains, part of the Rocky Mountain chain, extend into northern New Mexico. West of the mountains is the Colorado Plateau. Here wind and water have carved rock into canyons, arches, and other formations. Central and southern Arizona and New Mexico lie in the Great Basin. Mountains, **mesas**, and desert valleys make up this region. The deserts are dotted with cacti and other hardy plants.

The Rio Grande is the Southwest's longest river. It begins in the Rocky Mountains and runs south through New Mexico. Then it heads southeast to the Gulf of Mexico, marking the U.S.-Mexican border. The Red River forms part of the border between Oklahoma and Texas. Several other important rivers empty into the Gulf of Mexico. They include the Pecos and Brazos rivers.

The Colorado River cuts across northern Arizona and then turns south to form the Arizona-California border. On its way to the Gulf of California, it is joined by several **tributaries**, smaller rivers that feed into it. Among them are the Little Colorado and Gila rivers.

Rivers are very important to the Southwest. They provide water, and water is scarce in this part of the country. The Southwest, on average, gets little rain. The area is mild and dry in winter, and hot and dry in summer. Large parts of Arizona and New Mexico are true deserts, with as little as five inches of rain a year. With cooler temperatures and winter snows, mountain areas get enough moisture for pine forests to grow.

In contrast, eastern Texas shares the hot, humid climate of the South. Beaumont, in southeastern Texas, gets ten times as much rain as the Arizona deserts. Spring is the rainiest time of year. This is also the season for tornadoes. Texas and Oklahoma get their fair share of these violent storms.

The Colorado River runs through the Grand Canyon.

Coyotes, mule deer, bobcats, and smaller animals live in many parts of the Southwest. Endangered whooping cranes winter on the Texas coast. Desert animals are specially adapted to life in dry regions. They include lizards, snakes, armadillos, and the tiny kangaroo rat. The Southwest's high mountains are home to many large animals, including black bears, elk, and mountain lions.

Texas and Oklahoma have huge reserves of petroleum and natural gas. Arizona and New Mexico have rich deposits of silver and copper. These mineral resources have played an important role in the Southwest's growth, bringing many people to the region.

EARLY DAYS

Dreams of wealth brought Spanish explorers to the Southwest as early as 1539. They were seeking the fabled Seven Cities of Cibola, said to be built of gold. Instead, they found the pueblos of Indian groups who had lived in the Southwest for centuries.

Soon Spanish priests arrived, hoping to convert Indians to Christianity. Settlers followed. Santa Fe was founded in 1610 as the Spanish capital in New Mexico, as the region was called. Today it is the oldest seat of government in North America.

In 1680, the Pueblo Indians rebelled against Spain's harsh rule, and the Spanish

Ancient Pueblo Indian ruins (top). Pueblo Indian baking bread (above).

were forced out of New Mexico. They soon returned. By 1696, the Spanish were back in control. They also pushed into Texas. Spain ruled Texas and New Mexico until 1821, when Mexico won its independence. Then Mexico took over control.

Oklahoma's early days were different. The United States obtained most of the future state as part of the Louisiana Purchase in 1803. During the 1800s, it became Indian Territory. The Cherokees and other tribes, who were pushed off their land by white settlers, were given new land here.

 Think About It

How many years did Spain and Mexico control New Mexico? How is this history reflected in the region today?

MEXICO AND THE UNITED STATES

As soon as Mexico became independent, it opened its borders to trade with the United States. Soon American traders were bringing goods into New Mexico by way of the Santa Fe Trail. Mexico also agreed to let American settlers into Texas. Stephen F. Austin was the leader behind the new American settlements. By 1832, about 20,000 Americans had moved to Texas.

Sam Houston

Tensions soon grew between the new English-speaking settlers and the Mexican government. In 1836, the Texans declared independence. In a short but bloody war, they defeated the Mexican Army. The key battle took place at the San Jacinto River, on April 21. Texan Sam Houston led a surprise attack on the Mexicans and captured the Mexican leader Santa Anna.

Texas was an independent republic for ten years. Many more people from the United States moved to this new country. Then, in December 1845, Texas joined the Union as the 28th state. This angered Mexico, which still claimed the region.

Before long, a border dispute broke out. Mexico said that the Texas border was at the Sabine River. The United States said the border was at the Rio Grande, much farther south. In 1846, the two nations went to war.

The Mexican War ended with a U.S. victory in 1848. A peace treaty set the border at the Rio Grande River. It also gave the United States control of California and the territory of New Mexico. At that time, New Mexico included most of present-day Arizona and parts of Colorado and Nevada. The United States gained additional territory from Mexico in the Gadsden Purchase of 1854.

THE WILD SOUTHWEST

Texas left the Union and fought with the South during the Civil War (1861–1865). The war's end marked the start of a colorful period in the Southwest's history. Ranchers,

---

Focus On: The Alamo

The Alamo, in San Antonio, Texas, was the site of a famous battle in the Texas revolution. From February 23 to March 6, 1836, a band of about 180 Texas rebels held off the Mexican army here. Finally, the Mexicans launched a massive attack over the walls and took the fort. The defenders were all killed. Among the brave men who "held the fort" were the famous frontiersmen Jim Bowie and Davy Crockett. "Remember the Alamo" became a rallying cry for the Texans.

The Alamo

The Apache were one of the Southwest's Native American groups who suffered as white settlers took over the area's lands.

miners, and farmers came to the region in growing numbers. In Arizona and other areas, Indians fought to keep them out. By the 1870s, most of the Indians had been defeated. The Apache leader Geronimo was the last to surrender, in 1886.

English-speaking ranchers and farmers took the place of Mexican landowners, who had been the Southwest's leading citizens. The newcomers challenged one another for rights to land and scarce water. For a short time, the Southwest became the Wild West. Outlaws such as Billy the Kid (William H. Bonney) gained fame, and many disputes were settled with bullets.

By the 1880s, law and order had begun to take hold. Railroads linked most parts of the Southwest to the rest of the nation. The railroads made it easier to ship cattle and other products to market. Cowboys no longer had to drive herds overland to feed-lots in the Midwest.

Faced with growing demands for land, the U.S. government opened part of Indian Territory to white settlers in 1889. The result was a "land rush." Hundreds of settlers raced to stake claims. A series of similar land runs followed. Eventually, the Indian and white holdings were combined to form Oklahoma.

Oklahoma became a state in 1907. New Mexico and Arizona followed in 1912. They were the last of the "lower 48" states to join the Union.

THE "FIVE C'S"

The 20th century brought growth to the Southwest. The region thrived on the "five C's"—copper, crude oil, cattle, cotton, and citrus. New large-scale mining methods made Arizona the nation's leading copper producer. In 1901, oil was discovered at Spindletop, near Beaumont, Texas. The Spindletop "gusher" marked the start of a huge oil boom in Texas and Oklahoma. Houston and other ports on the Gulf of Mexico became centers for the oil industry.

Cattle and sheep ranching continued to be important. Farming grew after dams were built on the Rio Grande and other major rivers. The dams provided more water for irrigating farmland. Citrus fruits joined cotton and wheat as the region's most important crops. On the dry Oklahoma plains, farmers suffered during the great drought that produced the Dust Bowl of the 1930s. Today, better farming methods make such disasters less likely, but droughts are still a danger.

Dams have also provided water for cities and suburbs, and for manufacturing. South-western companies make everything from heavy machinery to electronic equipment. The Southwest has several major military and aerospace centers. Among them are the Johnson Space Center in Houston and Los Alamos National Laboratory, near Santa Fe.

Think About It

How has the damming of rivers changed life in the Southwest?

ARIZONA
Major industries: Electronic and aerospace equipment, machinery
Major farm products: Cattle, cotton, dairy products, lettuce

NEW MEXICO
Major industries: Electronics, analytical instruments, transportation equipment
Major farm products: Cattle, dairy products, hay, chili peppers

OKLAHOMA
Major industries: Industrial machinery, metal products, petroleum and coal products
Major farm products: Cattle, wheat, hogs, cotton

TEXAS
Major industries: Chemicals, petroleum products
Major farm products: Cattle, sorghum, cotton, wheat, rice

AZ
★ Phoenix

★ Santa Fe
NM

OK
★ Oklahoma City

TX

Austin ★

MAJOR CROPS AND INDUSTRIES OF THE SOUTHWEST

THE SOUTHWEST TODAY

The Southwest's growth has attracted job-seekers from all over. Many have come from northern states and from Mexico. Today a sixth "C"—climate—is helping the Southwest grow. Tourists and vacationers come to Arizona and New Mexico for the warm weather and spectacular scenery. Many people retire to this part of the country. Tourism and other service industries are now

Houston is the region's largest city.

YOUNG EXPLORER

Can you find Oklahoma on the map (page 52)?

How did mineral resources—oil, coal, silver, copper—affect the growth of the Southwest?

more important than mining or manufacturing to these states.

Houston, Texas, is the region's largest city. It has grown into the fourth-largest city in the United States. A ship channel links the city to the Gulf of Mexico, making it an important port. Skyscrapers and sprawling suburbs are features of Houston,

San Antonio, Texas

Focus On: The Grand Canyon

The Grand Canyon, in northern Arizona, ranks as one of the scenic wonders of the world. Over millions of years, the Colorado River washed away rock to carve this great gorge. The canyon is more than a mile deep and almost 280 miles long. Layers of sandstone, limestone, and lava create bands of color on its walls. The Grand Canyon was made a national park in 1919. Each year, millions of people visit it. Some hike down steep trails to the canyon floor. Some ride the rapids on the Colorado River. Many simply gaze in awe at the canyon's awesome natural beauty.

as well as Phoenix, Arizona, and other southwestern cities. Many towns still retain the flavor of the Old West. Among them is historic Santa Fe, New Mexico.

Oklahoma City became Oklahoma's state capital in 1910.

As more people have moved to the Southwest, water resources have been strained. The Southwest faces other problems, too. All groups have not shared equally in the region's boom. Poverty has been a problem for Mexican-Americans. It is also a problem on Indian reservations, such as the Hopi and Navajo reservations in northern Arizona.

Still, in many areas, Anglos (English-speakers), Native Americans, and Mexican-Americans are working together to solve these problems. The mixing of their cultures lends a special flavor to life in the Southwest.

CHAPTER REVIEW

1. The Sangre de Cristo Mountains are part of what mountain chain?
2. What southwestern states have large

The Southwest's 3 Largest Cities
(by population)

Houston, TX
1.7M

Phoenix, AZ
1.1M

San Antonio, TX
1.067M

reserves of petroleum and natural gas?

3. What did early Spanish explorers search for in the Southwest?

4. What city is the oldest seat of government in the United States?

5. Who led American settlers into Texas?

6. What did Texans do in 1836?

7. After the Mexican War, the Mexican-U.S. border followed what river?

8. Who was the last Southwestern Native American leader to give up the fight against white settlers?

9. When was Indian Territory (Oklahoma) first opened to white settlers?

10. What are the "five C's"?

11. What attractions bring tourists and vacationers to Arizona and New Mexico?

Activities

Here is a list of some famous people who were born or lived in the Southwest. Choose a person as a topic for a short report. Describe what your subject did and what was most important about his or her life. If possible, use the Internet for part of your research.

Arizona
ESTEVAN OCHOA, Political leader
SANDRA DAY O'CONNOR, U.S. Supreme Court justice
WILLIAM (BUCKY) O'NEILL, Frontier sheriff

New Mexico
CHRISTOPHER (KIT) CARSON, Trapper and scout
GEORGIA O'KEEFFE, Artist
POPE, Pueblo Indian leader

Oklahoma
WILMA MANKILLER, Cherokee leader
WILL ROGERS, Actor and humorist
MARIA TALLCHIEF, Ballerina

Texas
SAM HOUSTON, Soldier and statesman
LYNDON B. JOHNSON, U.S. president
BARBARA JORDAN, Politician and educator

FOCUS ON: Celebrating the Southwest

Here is a partial list of the many festivals and special events celebrated by towns and cities in the Southwest states. Choose one as the subject of a research paper. Then write about it in as much detail as possible.

ARIZONA
Cinco de Mayo
May 5, Nogales

La Fiesta de Los Vaqueros Rodeo
February, Tucson

NEW MEXICO
Hatch Chile Festival
September, Hatch

OKLAHOMA
Red Earth Native American Cultural Festival
June, Oklahoma City

TEXAS
Fiesta San Antonio
April, San Antonio

The Pacific States

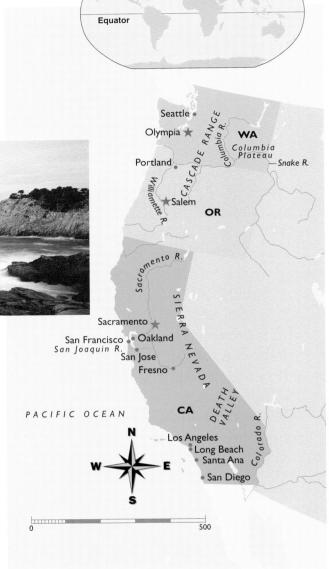

The Pacific Ocean pounds the West Coast of the United States for some 1,200 miles from Canada to Mexico. The states that share this long coastline make up one of the most varied regions in the country. Some of the tallest mountains in the United States are here. So is the country's lowest point—Death Valley, California, at 282 feet below sea level. The Pacific region has hot deserts, cool rain forests, and snow-capped volcanoes. In some places, cities sprawl over the land. In others, the wilderness is nearly untouched.

The Pacific shore at Point Lobos, California.

Waves pound the coast at Big Sur, California.

The people who live in this region have come from all over the country and the world.

The Pacific region includes three West Coast states: California, Oregon, and Washington. The Pacific Ocean also touches two other states—Alaska and Hawaii. These states are different from the West Coast states. Read about Alaska on pages 67-68, and about Hawaii on pages 69-70.

THE LAND

Some of the Pacific region's most important physical features lie deep underground. They are faults—breaks in the Earth's rocky crust. Motion along the fault lines produces earthquakes. Over millions of years, movement in the Earth's crust has also pushed up mountains along the Pacific coast.

Mountain chains run north-south through the West Coast states. The Cascade Range, in central Washington and Oregon, is made

AT A GLANCE

The Pacific States

CALIFORNIA
Area: 158,706 sq mi (411,049 km2)
Capital: Sacramento
Statehood: September 9, 1850; the 31st state
Motto: *Eureka* (I have found it).
Nickname: Golden State
Abbreviations: CA, Cal.
State bird: California valley quail
State flower: Golden poppy
State tree: Redwood

Asian 9% | Black 7% | White 58% | Hispanic and Other 26%

OREGON
Area: 97,073 sq mi (251,419 km2
Capital: Salem
Statehood: February 14, 1859; the 33rd state
Motto: *Alis volat propriis* (She flies with her own wings).
Nickname: Beaver State
Abbreviations: OR, Oreg.
State bird: Western meadowlark
State flower: Oregon grape
State tree: Douglas fir

Black 2% | Hispanic and Other 5% | White 93%

WASHINGTON
Area: 68,139 sq mi (176,479 km2)
Capital: Olympia
Statehood: November 11, 1889; the 42nd state
Motto: *Alki* (By and by).
Nickname: Evergreen state
Abbreviations: WA, Wash.
State bird: Willow goldfinch
State flower: Coast rhododendron
State tree: Western hemlock

Asian 4% | Hispanic and Other 4% | Black 3% | White 89%

up of volcanoes. Most of the volcanoes are quiet, but a few are still active. Among them is Mount St. Helens, in southern Washington. East of the Cascades, the dry uplands of the Columbia Basin cover Washington and Oregon.

South of the Cascades is the Sierra Nevada range. These rugged mountains continue into southern California, ending in the Mojave Desert. They include Mount Whitney, which is 14,495 feet above sea level— the tallest peak in any state except Alaska. The eastern slopes of the Sierras drop off sharply into desert basins.

Along the Pacific coast, the Coast Ranges run parallel to the Cascades and the Sierra Nevada. n many places these mountains meet the sea in sheer cliffs. In other places, narrow plains and sandy beaches face the ocean. Bays and inlets form excellent harbors at San Diego, San Francisco,

Mount Saint Helens is an active volcano in the Cascade Range.

and other points along the coast. Puget Sound, a long arm of the Pacific Ocean, reaches deep into western Washington.

Wide valleys lie between the Coast Ranges and the Cascades and Sierras. The Central Valley in California, the Willamette Valley in Oregon, and the Puget Sound Lowland in Washington are all important farming areas. Some of the Pacific region's most important rivers run through these valleys on their way to the ocean. They include the Sacramento and San Joaquin rivers in California and the Willamette River in Oregon.

The Columbia River is the most important river in the northwest. It runs along the Washington-Oregon border. The Columbia and its tributary, the Snake, have cut deep canyons in the Columbia Plateau. Hells Canyon, on the Snake River at the boundary between Oregon and Idaho, is the deepest gorge in North America.

The gorges cut by the Columbia River are some of the deepest in North America.

Cascade Mountains

Inland, valleys and eastern deserts bake in summer. The high mountains have freezing temperatures and heavy snows in winter.

Storms moving in off the Pacific bring lots of rain to the coast, especially in Washington and Oregon. The slopes of the Olympic Mountains, part of the Coast Ranges in Washington, are cloaked with evergreen rain forests. The western slopes of the Cascades and the Sierras also get plenty of rain and snow. Forests of Douglas fir, hemlock, cedar, and pine grow here. The California mountains have stands of giant sequoias, the world's largest trees, and California redwoods, the tallest trees. By the time air moves over high peaks of the Cascades and the Sierras, it has dumped most of its moisture. The eastern slopes of the mountains are dry.

The Cascades and Sierras are studded with lakes. Among the most famous is Lake Tahoe, on the California-Nevada border. The Salton Sea, in southern California, is a salt lake 235 feet below sea level.

"Sunny California" is famous for its mild climate. Year-round warmth and sunshine are mainly enjoyed in the southern part of that state. The Pacific region has many climate zones. Most areas along the coast have mild temperatures winter and summer.

California redwoods are among the world's tallest trees.

With so many climate zones, the Pacific region is home to a wide variety of wildlife. Deer, elk, black bears, bobcats, and coyotes are found in many areas. So are gophers, rattlesnakes, and other small animals. Mountain lions roam the eastern wilderness.

Forests and good soil are among the Pacific region's best resources. The Columbia and other rivers have been dammed to provide hydroelectric power and water reserves. A major oil field lies under the coastal mountains of California. The Sierras were the site of the famous California Gold Rush, but mining is no longer as important as it once was.

Father Junípero Serra (inset) founded California's first mission. Eventually missions, such as the one at San Gabriel (above), were built throughout California.

EARLY DAYS

The Spanish were the first Europeans to visit the West Coast. Beginning in the 1540s, Spanish ships explored the coast from the Gulf of California to what is now northern California. The English sea captain Francis Drake reached the coast of northern California in 1579. Many of these early explorers were searching for the Northwest Passage—a fabled shortcut from Europe to Asia.

The West Coast wasn't colonized until 1769, when the Spanish began founding settlements. They set up towns and forts at San Diego, Santa Barbara, San Francisco, and other points along the California coast. They also founded 21 missions, each about a day's journey apart, between San Diego and Sonoma. The goal of the missions was to convert Indians to Christianity. Spanish settlers were granted huge tracts of land, or ranchos, for raising cattle and other stock. The first mission was founded in 1769 by Father Junípero Serra.

While the Spanish were colonizing California, English and American explorers were scouting the Oregon region. Robert Gray was the first American to land on the Oregon coast, in 1788. Meriwether Lewis and William Clark traveled overland to the Pacific coast in 1805. Trappers and fur traders followed. Rival English and American fur companies started trading posts in the Oregon country. Britain and the United States controlled the region jointly until 1846.

FOCUS ON: Crater Lake

Crater Lake is the deepest lake in the United States—nearly 2,000 feet deep. This famous lake is located in southern Oregon, high in the Cascades. It lies in a caldera, the bowl of a huge volcano that blew apart in ancient times. The water's great depth makes it appear incredibly blue. Crater Lake National Park surrounds the lake. The park includes more than 250 square miles of spectacular forests and beautiful mountain meadows.

Crater Lake

YOUNG EXPLORER

Can you find Oregon on the map (page 60)?

Then they set the border between their lands at the 49th parallel of latitude.

American missionaries and settlers followed fur traders to Oregon. News of the area's rich soil and pleasant climate set off "Oregon fever" in the 1840s. Waves of settlers headed west by covered wagon to the Willamette Valley and other regions.

American traders and settlers also moved into California. The U.S. government tried several times to buy California, without success. In 1846, American settlers rebelled against Mexico in what became known as the Bear Flag Revolt. When the Mexican War broke out later that year, U.S. forces quickly occupied California. Mexico handed the territory over to the United States at the end of the war, in 1848.

GOLD FEVER

California was still thinly settled when it became part of the United States. There were about 10,000 Spanish-speaking Californians, and about 5,000 settlers and traders from the United States and other countries. Then, in 1848, gold was discovered at Sutter's Mill, on the American River. That set off a gold rush that brought tens of thousands of people. California's sleepy settlements became bustling cities almost overnight. Most of the newcomers were Americans. But people arrived from all over the world—even as far away as China. Some struck it rich in the gold fields. Others (like Levi Strauss) grew rich by selling supplies to miners.

People continued to flock to the Oregon country, too. In 1853, Washington was set up

Think About It

What drew settlers to the central valleys of the West Coast states?

as a separate territory north of the Columbia River. Gold was discovered in northeastern Washington in 1855. In 1858, gold was found along the Fraser River in Canada. Prospectors rushed through the territory, and new settlements grew quickly.

Whether they were headed for California or points north, pioneers and prospectors faced a hard journey. They crossed deserts and mountains. Sometimes they had to fend off outlaws and hostile Indians. The trip became much easier as railroads were built. The first transcontinental railroad was completed in 1869, with the help of Chinese workers. This and later railroad links helped farming and trade grow throughout the Pacific region.

Chief Joseph of the Nez Percé.

For Indians, however, the arrival of so many settlers brought hardship. They lost their lands, and their numbers declined. Some groups fought back. By the late 1870s, they had been defeated. The Nez Percé, led by Chief Joseph, were the last to give up the struggle.

WEST COAST GROWTH

In 1896, gold was discovered in Alaska and the Yukon Territory. Seattle became the jumping-off point for gold seekers headed there. Its population tripled in just ten years.

By this time, gold mining was no longer so important to California, but farms were

Focus On: The San Francisco Earthquake

On April 18, 1906, a powerful earthquake shook the city of San Francisco. The quake set off fires that burned for three days. About 2,500 people died, and almost 500 city blocks were destroyed. San Franciscans began to rebuild at once. By 1915, they were ready to show off their rebuilt city to the world by hosting the Panama–Pacific International Exposition.

San Francisco

prospering. California remained a land of opportunity—a place where people hoped to find a better life. Easterners continued to head west. A steady stream of immigrants also arrived from Mexico and from Japan and other Asian countries. Many new arrivals first found work as **migrant** farmhands, moving from place to place harvesting crops.

The 20th century brought more opportunities. Oil was discovered in southern California. The film industry took root in Hollywood, which soon became the nation's entertainment capital. The Pacific states also found ways to tap their precious water resources. In California, canals, aqueducts, dams, and reservoirs brought water to dry parts of the state. In Oregon and Washington, dams on the Columbia and other rivers provided hydroelectric power. With

plenty of water and electricity, farms and industries grew. West Coast port cities became centers of a thriving import-export trade.

During World War II, shipbuilding and airplane manufacturing became important industries. Washington became a producer of aluminum and materials for nuclear weapons and energy. The war years were a troubled time for the many Japanese-Americans of the Pacific region, however. After Japan attacked the U.S. naval base at Pearl Harbor, Hawaii, in December 1941, military authorities rounded up Japanese-Americans along the West Coast and sent them to camps. Citizens of Japanese ancestry were allowed to return to their homes in 1944.

Golden Gate Bridge

THE PACIFIC STATES TODAY

Because people have come to the Pacific states from so many parts of the world, this region has a lively cultural mix. Asian-Americans are an important part of most West Coast cities. California has many African Americans and Latinos.

The Pacific's 3 Largest Cities
(by population)

Los Angeles, CA
3,553,698

San Diego, CA
1,171,121

San Jose, CA
838,744

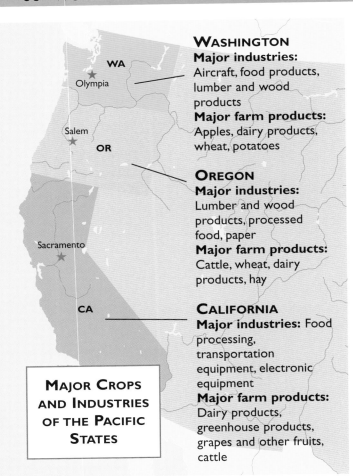

WASHINGTON
Major industries:
Aircraft, food products, lumber and wood products
Major farm products:
Apples, dairy products, wheat, potatoes

OREGON
Major industries:
Lumber and wood products, processed food, paper
Major farm products:
Cattle, wheat, dairy products, hay

CALIFORNIA
Major industries: Food processing, transportation equipment, electronic equipment
Major farm products:
Dairy products, greenhouse products, grapes and other fruits, cattle

MAJOR CROPS AND INDUSTRIES OF THE PACIFIC STATES

Downtown Seattle skyline

for the computer industry.

Oregon and Washington are leaders in producing timber products. And tourism is important throughout the Pacific region. People come from all over to visit this region's parks, wilderness areas, beaches, ski slopes, and lakes.

West Coast cities have seen amazing growth. Los Angeles is the region's biggest city. It is the center of a sprawling **metropolitan area** that includes about 75 cities and towns. San Diego, to the south, and San José and San Francisco, to the north, are California's next-largest cities. San Francisco is famous for its steep streets and cable cars. In recent years Portland, Oregon, and Seattle, Washington, have also seen rapid growth. Seattle, on the Puget Sound, is a major port. Its shipping links reach across the Pacific Ocean to Asia.

Growth has created many problems. Traffic jams, air pollution, and water shortages are among them. Some of California's urban centers have been troubled by tensions between whites and minority groups. Large numbers of illegal immigrants have caused strains in certain cities. Poor management has destroyed forests and other resources in some cities.

The people of the Pacific states are taking steps to solve these problems. They hope to preserve the natural beauty and attractions that have brought so many to this region.

People are still drawn to the West Coast by the promise of a better life, and there are plenty of opportunities. Almost every farm product, from avocados and citrus fruits to wheat and grapes for wine, is grown somewhere in the region. West Coast factories turn out automobiles, airplanes, televisions, and countless other products. The area around San Jose, California, is known as "Silicon Valley." It is an international center

Portland, Oregon

Los Angeles skyline

Alaska

AT A GLANCE

ALASKA

Area: 591,004 sq mi (1,530,700 km2)
Capital: Juneau
Statehood: January 3, 1959; the 49th state
Motto: "North to the future"
Nickname: Last Frontier
Abbreviations: AK
State bird: Willow ptarmigan
State flower: Forget-me-not
State tree: Sitka spruce

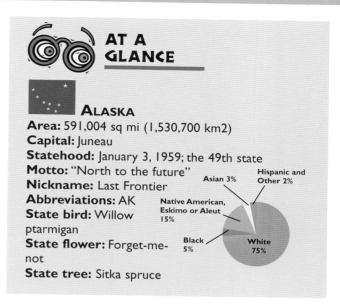

Asian 3%
Hispanic and Other 2%
Native American, Eskimo or Aleut 15%
Black 5%
White 75%

Alaska is so far north that a fourth of the state lies within the **Arctic Circle**. At its northernmost point, darkness lasts all day in winter. In summer, the sun never sets. Over the years, many fortune hunters have braved harsh conditions to find things like fur, gold, and oil in Alaska.

The northernmost U.S. state is also the biggest. It is more than twice as big as Texas, the next biggest state. It has more coastline than any other state. Alaska faces the Pacific Ocean to the south, the Bering Sea to the west, and the Arctic Ocean to the north. Among its roughly 1,000 islands are the Aleutians, which stretch far out into the Pacific. The farthest island is just 51 miles from Russia.

Mt. McKinley (Denali) in Alaska is the highest peak in the United States.

Caribou herd at a tundra waterhole.

A Harsh Land

Mountain ranges form a great arc through the southern part of Alaska. The Alaska Range has the highest peak in the United States—Mount McKinley (Denali), at 20,320 feet. Parts of southern Alaska get as much as 80 inches of snow in winter. The heavy snowfall helps feed glaciers, which are huge sheets of ice. Thick, evergreen forests cloak the lower mountain slopes.

The Brooks Range, part of the Rocky Mountain chain, rises in northern Alaska. North of the Brooks Range lies the Arctic Slope, or North Slope, a low coastal plain. Northern Alaska gets less snow than the south, but temperatures are colder. In the brief summers, only the top layer of ground thaws. **Permafrost**—permanently frozen ground—lies under much of the state.

Anchorage skyline (above). Fishing is a major industry in Alaska (left).

North of the Arctic Circle the land is covered by treeless tundra.

Despite its harsh climate, Alaska has a wonderful variety of wildlife. Herds of caribou roam the tundra. Grazing moose sometimes force Anchorage International Airport to close its runways. The state also has wolves and black, brown, grizzly, and polar bears. Alaska's fishing grounds are the richest in the nation.

Alaska's People

Alaska's native peoples—Inuits, Aleuts, and other groups—developed a way of life well suited to this harsh land. They survived by hunting, fishing, and gathering food during the short northern summers. Russian fur traders came to Alaska in the mid 1700s. They hunted fur seals and sea otters almost to extinction. After the fur trade declined, Russia sold Alaska to the United States for

$7.2 million in 1867. Many Americans thought the territory was worthless. Alaska soon turned out to have a lot to offer. The 1890s saw one gold strike after another, with major gold rushes in Klondike and Nome.

Alaska achieved statehood in 1959 and continued to grow. In 1968, a major oil field was discovered near Prudhoe Bay, on the Arctic Slope. Today, about a fifth of all petroleum produced in the United States comes from Alaska. Oil has brought wealth, but it has also brought environmental problems. The most serious came in 1989, when the oil tanker *Exxon Valdez* ran aground in Prince William Sound. Millions of gallons of crude oil spilled, harming birds, fish, and other animals.

Besides the oil industry, Alaskans today work in government and defense, mining, fishing, and other industries. Most live in and around the cities of Anchorage, Fairbanks, and Juneau. Many Alaskans, especially native peoples, still rely at least partly on hunting, fishing, and trapping. Much of Alaska is still untouched wilderness.

The Inuit are one of the native peoples from Alaska.

Hawaii

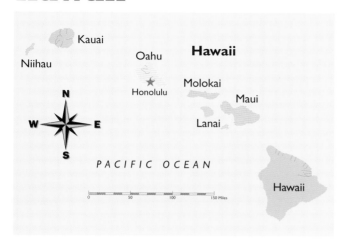

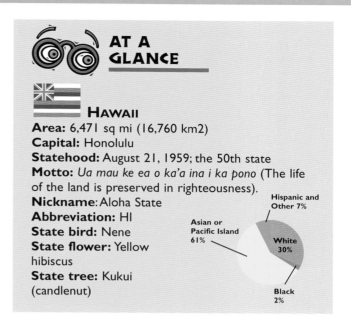

With balmy tropical weather and beautiful scenery, Hawaii seems close to paradise. This is the only one of the 50 U.S. states that isn't part of North America. Hawaii is made up of a chain of islands far out in the North Pacific Ocean. It is separated from the rest of the United States by about 2,400 miles of open water.

Hawaii is one of the smallest states. Only Rhode Island, Delaware, and Connecticut have less land. The islands that make up the state are strung out across the ocean for more than 1,500 miles.

Volcanic Islands

The Hawaiian Islands were formed by volcanoes on the ocean floor. Over millions of years, lava pouring from the volcanoes built up undersea mountains. Eventually, the mountains rose above the ocean surface.

Kilauea Crater, island of Hawaii

The mountaintops became the Hawaiian Islands. In the northwestern part of the island chain, the volcanoes stopped erupting long ago. Eruptions continued in the southeastern islands. The island of Hawaii, which is the largest in the chain, still has two active volcanoes. They are Kilauea and Mauna Loa.

Hawaii is one of eight main islands in the chain. The others are Maui, Kahoolawe, Lanai, Molokai, Oahu, Kauai, and Niihau. Each has its own character. Kauai has the wettest spot in the United States—Mount Waialeale, which gets 460 inches of rain a year. Many other areas on the islands are dry. Because it is so far from other land, Hawaii has many plants and animals found nowhere else.

The Hawaiians

The first Hawaiians came from other Pacific islands sometime before A.D. 1. They may have sailed from Tahiti in large oceangoing canoes. For hundreds of years, Hawaii was divided into several small kingdoms. Kamehameha I brought all the islands under his rule by 1805.

The attack on Pearl Harbor, 1941, brought the United States into World War II.

Island of Oahu

About that time, European and American ships began to stop at the islands. Traders, missionaries, and settlers soon followed, most from the United States. Planters arrived and founded large sugarcane plantations. They brought laborers from China, Japan, and other regions to work the land.

American influence grew steadily. In 1893, American planters and businessmen overthrew the Hawaiian monarchy. In the years that followed, people from Asia and Europe, as well as from America, settled in the islands. Hawaii became a U.S. territory in 1898 and the site of important military bases. A Japanese attack on the naval base at Pearl Harbor, on December 7, 1941, brought the United States into World War II.

Hawaii became a state in 1959. Since then, tourism has replaced farming as the most important part of the islands' economy. There are still big sugarcane and pineapple plantations and cattle ranches. Resort hotels line the islands' beautiful beaches, especially on Oahu. Housing developments cover much former farmland. Most Hawaiians live in towns and cities, especially in and around Honolulu, the state's capital. They are lucky to live in a state that's so close to paradise.

Hawaiian dancers

CHAPTER REVIEW

1. Where is the lowest point in the United States?
2. The Columbia River runs along the border of what two states?
3. What was the goal of the Spanish missions in California?
4. What set off "Oregon fever" in the 1840's?
5. The United States obtained California after what war?
6. When did the California Gold Rush begin?
7. Who was Chief Joseph?
8. What happened to West Coast Japanese-Americans during World War II?
9. What is the biggest city in the Pacific states?
10. What city is famous for its cable cars?
11. How much of Alaska is north of the Arctic Circle?
12. Which is the largest of the Hawaiian Islands?

Activities

Here is a list of some famous people who were born or lived in the Pacific states. Choose a person as a topic for a short report. Describe what your subject did and what was most important about his or her life.

Alaska
VITUS BERING, Russian explorer
JOSEPH JUNEAU, Prospector

California
GEORGE LUCAS, Filmmaker
SALLY K. RIDE, Astronaut

Hawaii
FATHER DAMIEN (JOSEPH DAMIEN DE VEUSTER), Missionary
LILIUOKALANI, Hawaiian queen

Oregon
BEVERLY CLEARY, Children's book author
ABIGAIL SCOTT DUNIWAY, Pioneer and suffragist

Washington
WILLIAM GATES III, Computer industry leader
SEATTLE, Suquamish Indian leader

FOCUS ON: Celebrating the Pacific States

Here is a partial list of the many festivals and special events celebrated by towns and cities in the Pacific states. Choose one as the subject of a research paper, using the Internet for part of your research.

ALASKA
Alaska Day
October, Sitka

CALIFORNIA
Tournament of Roses
January, Pasadena

HAWAII
Aloha Day
October, Oahu

OREGON
Rose Festival
June, Portland

WASHINGTON
Daffodil Festival
April, Puyallup

Toppenish Indian Powwow
July, Toppenish

When Americans rebelled against Britain in 1775, they wanted to free themselves from rule by the British king and parliament. They wanted a government that they would control themselves.

At the time, the idea that people should have a voice in government was still new. The Americans had few guidelines to follow, but they succeeded. The founders of the United States chose to form a **representative democracy**. In this system, the government is run by officials who are elected by the people, to represent the people.

The founders set out their ideas about government in three important documents. These documents form the foundation of the U.S. system. The system has worked well for more than 200 years. It has also become a model for many other countries.

Independence Hall, Philadelphia

THE DECLARATION OF INDEPENDENCE

In the spring of 1776, representatives of the thirteen colonies met in Philadelphia. Their purpose was to set out the reasons for their rebellion. The result was the creation of the Declaration of Independence. This document states some of the beliefs that led to the founding of the United States.

The Declaration can be divided into two parts. The first part outlines rights that the signers believed were held by all people. The second part sets out the ways in which the signers felt Britain's King George III had wronged the colonies. It is the first part that holds deepest meaning for Americans today. It also appeals to people worldwide, because the rights it sets out are universal.

The Declaration says that "all men are created equal." By this, it means that all people have the same rights. Kings and nobles should not enjoy greater rights than farmers and tradesmen. The Declaration goes on to state that all people are entitled to the right to life, to liberty, and to the "pursuit of happiness"—that is, to arrange their lives as they see fit.

The job of government, the Declaration says, is to protect these rights. When a government fails to do that, people should change it. Tyrants—rulers who would deny people their rights—should always be resisted. The Declaration also says that government should be based on the "consent of the governed." This was still a new idea in the 1700s. Back then, many countries were ruled by kings who

 **AT A GLANCE**

The U.S. Government

JUDICIAL BRANCH

SUPREME COURT, made up of the chief justice and eight associate justices (appointed for life by the president with Senate approval). **Role:** The nation's highest court; mainly hears appeals from lower courts. May declare laws unconstitutional, or invalid. **Other federal courts:** District courts (try cases involving federal laws); U.S. courts of appeal (hear appeals from district courts); special courts (hear cases involving taxes, the military, and international trade).

EXECUTIVE BRANCH

PRESIDENT (elected for a 4-year term). **Role:** Ensures that laws are carried out; acts as head of state (the country's leading representative) and commander in chief of armed forces; may reject (veto) legislation. **Reporting to the president:** Cabinet departments (State, Treasury, Defense, Justice, Interior, Agriculture, Commerce, Labor, Health and Human Services, Housing and Urban Development, Transportation, Energy, Education, Veterans Affairs), National Security Council, other executive agencies.

LEGISLATIVE BRANCH

UNITED STATES CONGRESS, made up of the Senate (100 members elected for 6-year terms) and House of Representatives (435 members elected for 2-year terms). **Role:** Makes laws, funds government programs, may declare war, may impeach (bring charges against) members of other branches of government. **Reporting to Congress:** Library of Congress, Congressional Budget Office.

claimed to rule by "divine right." That is, they said their powers were granted by God.

Americans have not always lived up to the words of the Declaration. Many of the signers kept slaves, and they did not think women should have the same rights as men. Over the years, the United States has moved closer to the ideals set out in the Declaration of Independence.

Dome of the Capitol, Washington, D.C.

 Think About It

Do you think the United States still falls short of the ideals set out in the Declaration of Independence? If so, in what ways?

THE CONSTITUTION

At first, Americans were worried about giving too much power to a central government. The states formed a very loose union, under a document called the Articles of Confederation. State governments kept most powers for themselves.

This arrangement didn't work well. Congress had so little power that it couldn't enforce laws. It couldn't even raise money to pay the country's debts. States argued over borders and trade. The new country seemed likely to fall apart.

In 1787, representatives from the states met in Philadelphia and wrote a new Constitution. This document set up the framework for the U.S. government as it is

Focus On: Thomas Jefferson (1743-1826)

When colonial representatives decided to declare independence in 1776, they assigned Thomas Jefferson of Virginia the job of writing the declaration. He wrote out a draft with his quill pen, on a portable desk he had designed himself. Others helped craft the final version. The words of the Declaration of Independence are mainly Jefferson's.

Jefferson later became the third U.S. president. He also served as minister to France, secretary of state, vice president, and governor of Virginia. He was an inventor and a self-taught architect. He studied nature, language, and other subjects. He did not want any of these things mentioned on his tombstone. He wanted to be remembered for three things. First was the Declaration of Independence. Second was Virginia's law guaranteeing religious freedom, which he also wrote. Third was the University of Virginia, which he founded.

today. The United States has a **federal system**. That is, the national government shares power with the state governments. The Constitution provides for a national government that is strong but democratic.

To prevent any abuse of power, the authors of the Constitution set up a system of "checks and balances." Under this system, powers are divided among three branches: legislative, executive, and judicial. No one branch has too much power on its own, and each branch depends on the cooperation and supervision of the other branches.

The legislative branch—the U.S. Congress—writes laws. Congress raises money for the government, through taxes, and decides how to spend it. Only Congress can declare war.

Congress has two houses. The Senate has 100 members—two for each state—who are elected for 6-year terms. The House of Representatives has 435 members, elected for 2-year terms. Seats in the house are divided up according to the population of the states, with big states getting more.

The executive branch carries out laws. The president, who is elected for a 4-year term, heads the executive branch. This job carries many

George Washington presided over the Constitutional Convention in Philadelphia, 1787.

Think About It

How does a democratic system of government help provide people with opportunities for a good life?

responsibilities. Besides ensuring that laws are carried out, the president proposes new laws and programs. He or she may veto, or reject, laws passed by Congress.

The president is also the commander in chief of the armed forces. In this way, the Constitution specifically puts the U.S. military under civilian control. The president is also the U.S. chief of state. In this role, he or she meets with leaders of other nations. The fact that the chief of state is elected makes the United States a republic.

The judicial branch reviews laws and the way in which they are carried out. The nation's top court is the U.S. Supreme Court. Its members—a chief justice and eight associate justices—are appointed by the president, with the approval of the Senate. They serve for life, or until they choose to retire. The Supreme Court hears cases appealed from lower courts. It has the power of judicial review. This means that it can strike down laws by declaring them unconstitutional. In this way, the Supreme Court can check the power of the president and Congress, and of state governments.

The 50 state governments have the same structure as the federal government. They, too, have three branches—a legislature, an executive (governor), and state courts.

THE BILL OF RIGHTS

When the Constitution was proposed, many people worried that the new national

Focus On: Benjamin Franklin (1706-1790)

Delegates to the Constitutional Convention of 1787 didn't always see eye to eye. When they disagreed, they often turned to Benjamin Franklin. Franklin was 81 and too weak to stand. His mind was sharp. His opinions were respected by all.

Franklin had been a successful printer and writer in Philadelphia. His *Sayings of Poor Richard* made him rich and famous. It was filled with advice and sayings, such as "Little strokes fell great oaks" and "Fish and visitors stink after three days." Franklin had many other interests, too. He carried out scientific experiments involving electricity. He developed inventions such as the Franklin stove and bifocal glasses. He also served as the first postmaster for the colonies.

As the United States took shape, Franklin was involved in every step. He was on the committee that helped Thomas Jefferson write the Declaration of Independence. He helped win support from France for the Revolutionary War. He helped work out the terms of the treaty that ended the war, and he was one of three Americans who signed it.

After he helped write the Constitution, Franklin urged the states to approve it. He died confident that the new nation was headed in the right direction.

government might take away the rights they had fought for in the Revolutionary War. Several states refused to ratify (approve) the Constitution until they were promised that guarantees of rights would be added to it.

The first Congress of the new government met in 1789. And amending (changing) the Constitution was the first order of business. Congress passed twelve **amendments** to the Constitution. Ten were approved by the states and took effect in 1791. Those amendments became known as the Bill of Rights.

- **The First Amendment** prevents Congress from limiting some very important rights. Those rights are freedom of religion, freedom of speech, freedom of the press, the right to assemble, and the right to petition the government.
- **The Second Amendment** says that because a "well-regulated **militia**" is necessary for a free state, the government may not prevent the people from keeping arms (weapons). This amendment reflects the important role played by citizen-soldiers in the Revolutionary War.
- **The Third Amendment** says that government can't lodge soldiers in private homes, except in wartime. This reflects a concern from colonial times, when British troops were quartered in American homes.
- **The Fourth Amendment** says that government must have a warrant—a document signed by a judge—before it can seize people's possessions or search their homes for evidence of crimes. The government must convince the judge that there is good reason to make the search.

Think About It

Why are freedom of speech and of the press important in a democracy?

- **The Fifth Amendment** protects people who are accused of crimes. It says that, for serious crimes, charges must be brought by a grand jury. It protects people from being tried twice on the same charge or forced to testify against themselves. It also says that government can't take private property without paying a fair price for it. It guarantees everyone "due process of law"—the right to fair legal treatment.
- **The Sixth Amendment** gives people accused of crimes the right to a speedy and public trial by jury. The accused have the right to know what crimes they are charged with, to be confronted with the witnesses against them, and to have a lawyer defend them.
- **The Seventh Amendment** guarantees the right to jury trials in civil cases (lawsuits).
- **The Eighth Amendment** prohibits excessive bail or fines or cruel and unusual punishments.
- **The Ninth Amendment** says that people keep any rights that are not named in the Constitution.
- **The Tenth Amendment** says that any powers not specifically given to the federal government by the Constitution are held by the states or by the people.

The Constitution has been amended sixteen more times since 1791, for a variety of reasons. Each amendment has allowed the Constitution to meet the country's changing needs. The Bill of Rights, however, remains a cornerstone of American democracy.

CHAPTER REVIEW

1. Why did representatives of the thirteen colonies meet in Philadelphia in 1776?
2. What is a tyrant?
3. Why did the American states form a very loose union at first?

Focus On: James Madison (1751-1836)

James Madison is sometimes called the "Father of the Constitution." More than anyone, he helped shape the final document. He was also the main author of the Bill of Rights.

A Virginian, Madison was 25 when the Revolutionary War began. He wasn't strong enough to serve in the army, so he turned to public affairs. He soon became a leading member of the Continental Congress. After the war, he led the drive to strengthen the weak government set up under the Articles of Confederation.

Madison came up with the outline of the plan that was adopted at the Constitutional Convention of 1787. It was his idea to have three branches of government: a strong president, a legislature with two houses, and an independent court system.

Madison went on to have a long career in government. He served in Congress, as secretary of state, and as the fourth U.S. president. Despite his long political career, he is most famous for his work on the Constitution and on the Bill of Rights.

4. The Constitution divides power among what three branches of government?
5. Which branch raises money for the government?
6. Who commands the U.S. armed forces?
7. How long to Supreme Court justices serve?
8. How many amendments are in the Bill of Rights?
9. What rights are protected by the First Amendment?
10. Under the Ninth Amendment, who holds rights not named in the Constitution?

Activities

Besides the people profiled in the chapter, many people helped shape American government. Here is a list of some of some of the people involved in creating the Declaration of Independence, the Constitution, and the Bill of Rights. Choose one for a brief report. Explain what your subject did and why he was important.

- JOHN ADAMS, Massachusetts
- SAMUEL ADAMS, Massachusetts
- SAMUEL CHASE, Maryland
- WILLIAM ELLERY, Rhode Island
- ELBRIDGE GERRY, Massachusetts
- BUTTON GWINNETT, Georgia
- ALEXANDER HAMILTON, New York
- JOHN HANCOCK, Massachusetts
- PATRICK HENRY, Virginia
- JOHN JAY, New York
- GEORGE MASON, Virginia
- GOUVERNOUR MORRIS, Pennsylvania
- LEWIS MORRIS, New York
- CAESAR RODNEY, Delaware
- EDWARD RUTLEDGE, South Carolina
- ROGER SHERMAN, Connecticut
- RICHARD STOCKTON, New Jersey
- MATTHEW THORNTON, New Hampshire
- GEORGE WASHINGTON, Virginia

Canada

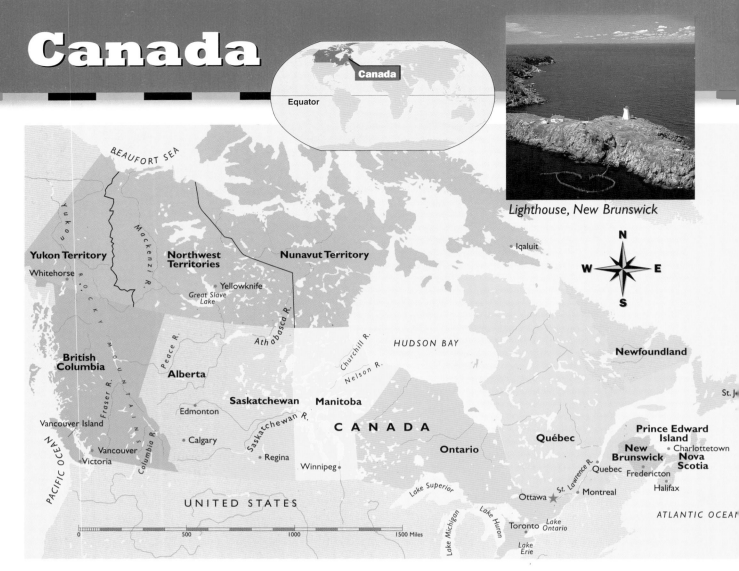

Lighthouse, New Brunswick

Hardwood forest, Québec

What is the largest country in North America? It's Canada, the northern neighbor of the United States. Canada takes up most of the northern half of the continent. In all the world, only Russia has a larger land area.

Canada stretches from sea to sea...to sea. It borders the Atlantic Ocean in the East, the Pacific Ocean in the west, and the Arctic Ocean in the north. It has more coastline than any other country. Canada's northernmost point is just 500 miles from the North Pole. To the south, the U.S.-Canadian border runs for more than 5,500 miles. Canada also borders U.S. territory in the northeast, where Alaska is its next-door neighbor.

Within Canada's boundaries are ten provinces and three territories. Like the states of the United States, each of these divisions has a flavor all its own.

THE LAND

Canada has broad plains and towering mountain ranges. In the north, forests give way to treeless stretches of **tundra**. Much of the country is still wilderness. With a harsh climate and poor soils, northern Canada isn't suitable for farming. Most Canadians live in

AT A GLANCE **Canada**

Official name: Canada
Capital: Ottawa
Area: 3,851,794 sq mi (9,976,140 km2)
Population: 28,846,761
Form of government: Constitutional monarchy
Provinces (capital cities in brackets): Alberta (Edmonton); British Columbia (Victoria); Manitoba (Winnipeg); New Brunswick (Fredericton); Newfoundland (St. John's); Nova Scotia (Halifax); Ontario (Toronto); Prince Edward Island (Charlottetown); Québec (Québec City); Saskatchewan (Regina);
Territories (capital cities in brackets) Northwest Territories (Yellowknife); Nunavut (Iqaluit); Yukon Territory (Whitehorse)
Major farm products: Livestock, dairy products, wheat
Major industries: Paper and wood products, motor vehicles, petroleum products, meat products
Natural resources: Petroleum and natural gas, nickel, zinc, uranium
Unit of money: Canadian dollar
Major languages: English, French (both official)
Major religions: Roman Catholic, Protestant, Jewish, Muslim

Other European 20%
Indigenous Indian, Eskimo and Asian 13%
British Isles 40%
French 27%

the south, within a few hundred miles of the U.S. border.

Canada has seven major regions:

- The Appalachian region is in the east. This area is an extension of the Appalachian Mountains, which run

Wheat fields cover the plains of Saskatchewan.

through eastern North America. It includes Canada's Atlantic provinces— New Brunswick, Nova Scotia, Prince Edward Island, and Newfoundland. Low, rugged hills and fertile valleys cover much of the region. The coastline is jagged, with many bays. Off the east coast of Newfoundland is the famous fishing ground known as the Grand Banks.

Canadian Rockies

- The Great Lakes—St. Lawrence Lowlands include southern Québec and Ontario. Half of all Canadians live in this region, around the Great Lakes and the St. Lawrence River. Canada's two largest cities, Montreal and Toronto, are here. There are also many farms. In spring, groves of sugar maples are tapped to produce maple syrup and sugar. The trees also give Canada its national symbol, the maple leaf.

- The Canadian Shield makes up much of the heart of Canada. The shield is a rocky region that surrounds Hudson Bay, a huge inland sea that reaches deep into northern Canada. Here, the land was shaped and scraped by ancient glaciers. Some of the rocks are more than 3 billion years old. Most parts of this region have only a thin layer of poor soil. Evergreen forests grow, but the soil isn't rich enough for farming.

- The Prairie Provinces are Alberta, Saskatchewan, and Manitoba. Here, fields of wheat roll on almost endlessly. The Prairies are part of the North American

Think About It

Can you think of reasons why most Canadians live in the southern part of the country?

Grain harvesting in Alberta.

Great Plains. They are among the richest grain-producing regions in the world. But the land is not all flat. In Alberta's Red Deer River Valley, for example, water and wind have carved sandstone into strange shapes called "hoodoos." Many dinosaur fossils have been found in this region.

• The Cordillera lies west of the Prairies. It covers western Alberta and most of British Columbia. Here the land rises to the snow-covered peaks of the Canadian Rockies, the Coastal Mountains, and other ranges. The mountain ranges run north to south. Between them are deep, dry valleys. Canada's highest peaks are in the St. Elias range. This range is an extension of the Coast Mountains that reaches into the Yukon Territory. The highest of all is Mount Logan, at 19,524 feet.

• The Pacific Coast is cut by deep inlets, called fiords. Vancouver Island and the Queen Charlotte Islands lie offshore, sheltering the mainland from storms. Between the islands and the mainland is a natural waterway, the Inland Passage. Ancient forests of western red cedar and Douglas fir cloak the mountains on the islands and along the coast.

• The Arctic region includes most of the Northwest Territories and Nunavut. Here, a maze of islands stretches from the north coast into the Arctic Ocean. Cape Columbia, on Ellesmere Island, is Canada's northernmost point. The Arctic is a region of harsh beauty. During the short summers, daylight lasts nearly around the clock. Wildflowers bloom on the tundra. The winters are long and dark, with subzero temperatures.

Seen from the air, parts of Canada seem to have more water than land. There are

Focus On: Banff National Park

Jagged peaks, glaciers, alpine meadows, crystal lakes, and mineral hot springs are some of the wonderful natural features protected in Banff National Park. The park is located on the eastern slopes of the Rocky Mountains in in the province of Alberta. Established in 1885, it is Canada's oldest national park. Today, it covers an area larger than the state of Delaware. Elk, bighorn sheep, black and grizzly bears, caribou, and many other animals roam freely within the park.

Peyto Lake, Banff National Park

some 2 million lakes in the country. Canada shares four of the Great Lakes—Huron, Superior, Erie, and Ontario-with the United States. The largest lake entirely within Canada is Great Slave Lake, in the Northwest Territories.

The St. Lawrence is Canada's most important river. The St. Lawrence Seaway provides a route for ships from the Great Lakes to the Atlantic Ocean. The longest Canadian river is the Mackenzie, which flows through the Northwest Territories to Great Slave Lake. The Nelson, Churchill, Saskatchewan, Peace, and Athabasca are among the major rivers of central Canada. Large rivers in the west include the Yukon, the Fraser, and the Columbia, which flows partly through U.S. territory.

Canada's climate ranges from harsh to mild. The northernmost islands have ice year-round. But coastal British Columbia is warmed by moist air moving off the Pacific Ocean. It has a moderate climate with lots of rain.

Most of rest of the country has a true four-season climate, with cold winters and warm summers. The farther north you go, the colder winter is—and the longer it lasts. Mountain regions and the eastern provinces get the most snow—65 inches or more each winter. In the plains, bitter winter cold is sometimes broken by the chinook, a warm wind that blows from the west.

Forests and other wooded areas cover almost 50 percent of Canada's land area. In fact, Canada has 10 percent of the world's forests, and timber is one of its most important resources. The Prairies have large deposits of crude oil and natural gas. The rocky Canadian Shield holds rich deposits of minerals, including gold, silver, zinc, copper, and uranium.

With so much wilderness, Canada is home to many wild animals. Elk, deer, and moose roam the forests. Beavers live along the streams. Black and grizzly bears, wolves, foxes, and coyotes are common. Herds of caribou range across the tundra. Polar bears prowl the Arctic ice. Arctic waters are home to seals and walruses, as well as many fish.

EARLY DAYS

Before Europeans arrived, many different Indian and Inuit groups lived in the regions that are part of Canada today. The first Europeans any of these people met were probably Vikings, who sailed west from Iceland around A.D. 1000. They settled on Newfoundland, but they stayed only a short time. Europeans didn't really begin to explore Canada for another 500 years.

Beginning around 1500, explorers such as John Cabot—who sailed for England—and the French Jacques Cartier and Samuel de Champlain first arrived in Canada. They were looking for the Northwest Passage,

English explorers John and Sebastian Cabot arrived in Canada about 1500.

a fabled shortcut to the Far East. They never found it, but they did find the rich fishing grounds of the Grand Banks. They soon discovered that Canada's forests teemed with beavers and other valuable fur-bearing animals.

The French built forts and fur-trading posts along the St. Lawrence River and around the Great Lakes. The British did likewise around Hudson Bay and along the Atlantic coast. Settlements grew steadily. So did rivalry between the French and the British. Indians who wanted to profit from the fur trade were caught up in the rivalry. The Iroquois were the most powerful allies of the English, while the Huron and Algonquin sided with the French.

The dispute was finally settled in the French and Indian War, which broke out in the 1750s. In 1759, the British captured the French fortress at Québec. The next year, French forces surrendered at Montreal and the colony of New France came under British rule. The people who lived there were allowed to keep their own language, customs, religion, and legal system.

BRITISH CANADA

When America's Revolutionary War broke out in 1775, Canadian colonists stayed loyal to Britain. Many Loyalists moved from the United States to Canada during and after the war. With the population growing, Britain reorganized its holdings in 1791. English-speaking Upper Canada (now Ontario) was established separately from French-speaking Lower Canada (Québec).

As separate British colonies, Upper and Lower Canada, Nova Scotia, New Brunswick, Prince Edward Island, and Newfoundland continued to grow. When war broke out between Britain and the United States in 1812, the British drove back American attacks

Think About It

How do Canada's two official languages, English and French, reflect the country's history?

in Canada. In Pacific Northwest, the British and Americans argued over control of the Oregon Territory. They settled the issue without a fight in 1848. In that year, the Oregon Treaty fixed the border between British Columbia and the United States.

All the same, people had begun to worry that the colonies might eventually be absorbed by the United States. The best way to prevent that, they decided, was to form a union. In 1867, under the British North America Act, Upper and Lower Canada joined with Nova Scotia and New Brunswick to form the Dominion of Canada. British Columbia joined in 1871, and Prince Edward Island in 1873. The new country was self-governing in everything except foreign affairs. It remained part of the British Empire.

CANADA GROWS

Between Canada's eastern provinces and British Columbia were vast lands owned by the Hudson's Bay Company, which controlled the fur trade. Trappers, hunters, and traders lived in scattered settlements. This

YOUNG EXPLORER

Can you find the Prairie Provinces—Alberta, Saskatchewan, and Manitoba—on the map (page 78)?

Why do you think they resemble the Great Plains of the United States?

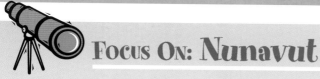

Focus On: Nunavut

Nunavut, Canada's newest territory, was created on April 1, 1999. "Nunavut" means "our land" in Inuktitut, an Inuit language. The Inuit make up about 85 percent of Nunavut's people.

Nunavut is huge—bigger than Alaska and California combined. It was carved from the Northwest Territories to settle a dispute over land claimed by the Inuit. Rocky islands make up most of the territory. During the long winters, they are linked by thick ice.

Only about 22,000 people live in this harsh land. Caribou outnumber people by more than 25 to 1! There are just 28 towns and villages. Iqaluit, the capital, on Baffin

Baffin Island

Island, is the largest. Jobs are hard to come by, but this part of the world is the traditional Inuit homeland. Many of today's Inuit still hunt and fish, as their ancestors did. This helps them to survive.

region, which was known as Rupert's Land, included many Indians and metis, people of Indian-French descent.

Canada bought these lands in 1870. The people who lived there objected to the transfer. They also feared that as settlers moved into the region, they would lose their traditional way of life. Louis Riel, a metis, became their leader. In 1885, he led the Indians and metis in an uprising known as the Northwest Rebellion. The rebellion was crushed, and Riel was executed. English-speaking Canadians viewed him as a traitor. To French Canadians, he was a hero.

In 1896, gold was discovered along the Klondike River in the far northwest. Miners rushed to the region. Boomtowns sprang up overnight. To keep control of the region, Canada established the Yukon Territory. The gold rush was soon over, but Canada continued to grow. By the late 1800s, its east and west coasts were linked by railroads. Settlers moved to the plains to farm and raise livestock. In 1905, two new provinces

were carved from Rupert's Land: Alberta and Saskatchewan. The rest of the land became Northwest Territories.

Canadians fought in World War I and World War II on the side of Britain and the United States. Between the wars, Canada gained recognition as a fully independent nation. After World War II, it welcomed a wave of immigrants. More than 4 million people immigrated to Canada from other countries between 1951 and 1981. Most came from Europe and the United States.

Many of the new arrivals settled in Ontario, where industry was growing. Others, especially those from Eastern Europe, headed west. They became farmers, ranchers, or workers in the new oil industry.

The map of Canada didn't take its present form until 1999. Newfoundland remained a British colony until 1949, when it became Canada's tenth province. In 1999, the northern territory of Nunavut was carved from the Northwest Territories.

Toronto, Ontario

CANADA TODAY

Today, Canadians enjoy the world's sixth-highest standard of living. Farming, forestry, and mining are still important. But manufacturing—of automobiles, pulp and paper, iron and steel, machinery and equipment—has grown. More than three out of four Canadians live in cities and towns. Toronto, Montreal, Vancouver, and the combined city of Ottawa-Hull are the largest cities. Ottawa is the national capital.

Canada's government is based on the British system. Like Britain, it is a **constitutional monarchy**. A governor-general (representing the British monarch) is head of state, but has no real power. The government is headed by a prime minister, who is the leader of the party that commands a majority in Parliament. Parliament consists of the House of Commons and the Senate. Parliament makes laws in areas that affect the nation as a whole, such as defense. Provincial governments are in charge of education and regional affairs.

Canada's heritage is reflected in the fact that it has two official languages: English and French. French is the

Québec City

first language of most people in Québec. But English and French aren't the only languages spoken in Canada. Immigrants from many lands have brought many tongues—Chinese, Italian, German, Polish, Spanish, Ukrainian, Arabic, Dutch, and Greek, to name a few. Canada's native peoples—the cultural grouping of Eskimo, Aleut, Athabascan and Algonquin—make up about three percent of the population. Many of them still speak their native languages.

Canadians have much in common, from a shared history to a passion for ice hockey. The many ethnic groups mostly get along, making a wonderful patchwork of cultures. Canadians have also had to grapple with some basic questions about their nation. Many French-speaking people in Québec think their province should have greater independence from Canada. Québec has voted on this question twice, in 1980 and 1995. Both times, a majority voted to remain a province of Canada.

In 1982, Canada revised its constitution and adopted a new Charter of Rights and Freedoms. Canadians are proud of this charter. It guarantees many basic rights, such as freedom of speech. It also protects the rights of native peoples and Canada's many other ethnic groups.

Parliament Hill, Ottawa

Vancouver, British Columbia

CHAPTER REVIEW

1. What three oceans does Canada border?
2. Where is Hudson Bay?
3. What is Canada's northernmost point?
4. Who were the first Europeans in Canada?
5. Where did the French build forts and fur-trading posts?
6. With whom did Canadians side during the American Revolutionary War?
7. When was the Dominion of Canada formed?
8. What was the Northwest Rebellion?
9. What Canadian territory was created in 1999?
10. Whom does Canada's governor-general represent?

Activities

Here is a list of some famous Canadians. Choose a subject for a brief report. Explain what your subject did and why he or she was important. If possible, use the Internet for part of your research.

FREDERICK GRANT BANTING, Doctor and scientist
KIM CAMPBELL, Prime minister
JIM CARREY, Comedian
JACQUES CARTIER, French explorer
ADRIENNE CLARKSON, Governor-general
GLENN GOULD, Musician
WILLIAM LYON MACKENZIE KING, Prime minister
RENE LEVESQUE, Québec political leader
J.E.H. MACDONALD, Artist
SIR ALEXANDER MACKENZIE, Fur trader and explorer
LOUISE CRUMMY MCKINNEY, Suffragist and legislator
AGNES MCPHAIL, Political leader
LUCY MAUD MONTGOMERY, Author
MARY PICKFORD, Silent film star
LOUIS RIEL, Metis leader
EMILY JENNINGS STOWE, Doctor
PIERRE ELLIOTT TRUDEAU, Prime minister

FOCUS ON: Celebrating Canada

Here is a partial list of the many festivals and special events celebrated by towns and cities in Canada. Choose one as the subject of a research paper. Then write about it in as much detail as possible.

Nova Scotia International Tattoo
July, Halifax, Nova Scotia

Quebec Winter Carnival
February, Québec City, Québec

London International Children's Festival
June, London, Ontario

Canada's National Ukrainian Festival
August, Dauphin, Manitoba

Pion-Era
July, Saskatoon, Saskatchewan

Calgary Stampede
July, Calgary

FolkFest
July, Victoria, British Columbia

Great Klondike International Outhouse Race
September, Dawson City, Yukon Territory

Midnight Madness
June, Inuvik, Northwest Territories

Mexico

Mexico

Equator

UNITED STATES

Baja California Norte

Sonora

Chihuahua

SIERRA MADRE OCCIDENTAL

Coahuila

Rio Grande R.

Nuevo Leon

Monterrey

Gulf of Mexico

GULF OF CALIFORNIA

Baja California Sur

Durango

Sinaloa

Zacatecas

CENTRAL PLATEAU

SIERRA MADRE ORIENTAL

Tamaulipas

MEXICO

San Luis Potosi

1. Aguascalientes
2. Guanajuato
3. Queretaro
4. Hidalgo
5. Mexico
6. Distrito Federal
7. Morelos
8. Tlaxcala

Merida   Cancun

Yucatán

Pacific Ocean

Nayarit

1

2

Guadalajara

3   4

Quintana Roo

Jalisco

Mexico City

5 6 8

Campeche

Colima   Michoacan

5 7 Puebla

Veracruz   Tabasco

Guerrero

Acapulco   Oaxaca

Chiapas

N W E S

0   100   200   300   400   500 Miles

Aztec stone carving

 In the heart of Mexico City is a great square, the Plaza of Three Cultures. The three cultures are those of the Indians, the Spanish, and modern Mexico. The Mayas, Aztecs, and other Indians of Mexico built great civilizations long before Europeans reached America. The Spanish conquered them and ruled for hundreds of years. Modern Mexico has also drawn on its Indian and Spanish heritage to create a culture all its own.

THE LAND

Mexico is about a fifth as large as the United States, its northern neighbor. From the U.S. border, it runs south and east to Belize and Guatemala. It is a country of great contrasts—with snow-capped volcanoes, steamy jungles, and barren deserts.

Coast near Cabo San Lucas, Baja

Beaches and tropical rain forests line Mexico's coasts. The eastern coast begins at the mouth of the Rio Grande River, at the U.S. border. It curves south and east around the Gulf of Mexico to the Yucatán Peninsula. Here thick jungles guard the ruins of ancient Mayan temples.

AT A GLANCE — Mexico

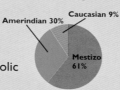

Official name: United Mexican States
Capital: Mexico City
Area: 761,600 sq mi (1,972m547 km2)
Population: 95,700,000
Form of government: Federal republic
Major farm products: Corn, beans, wheat, cotton, coffee
Major industries: Motor vehicles, food processing, metals, chemical products
Natural resources: Petroleum and natural gas, silver, copper
Unit of money: Peso
Major language: Spanish (official)
Major religion: Roman Catholic

Amerindian 30%   Caucasian 9%
Mestizo 61%

Fisherman returning home to Puerto Vallarta.

Bowls in an outdoor market.

Mexico's western coast faces the Pacific Ocean. Baja California (Lower California), a long peninsula, juts down from the north. Between the peninsula and the mainland is the Gulf of California. It was once called the Sea of Cortés for Hernando Cortés, who first explored it in 1536.

Two major mountain ranges march down the length of Mexico. They are the Sierra Madre Oriental, in the east, and the Sierra Madre Occidental, in the west. The two mountain ranges form a V, with its base pointing south. Between them is a high, wide plateau. This Central Plateau is Mexico's heartland. It has the country's best farmland and most of its major cities. Mexico City, the capital, is in the southern part of the plateau.

Near Mexico City is Mexico's highest mountain, Citlaltepetl. This snowcapped volcano stands 18,700 feet above sea level. South of Mexico City are more mountains— the Sierra Madre del Sur—and highland regions.

FOCUS ON: Popocatépetl

Popocatépetl is Mexico's second-highest mountain—and its most famous volcano. It's in central Mexico, just 45 miles from Mexico City. After erupting violently in the 1920s, Popocatépetl was quiet for 70 years. In the mid-1990s, the mountain began to wake up. Since then, it has regularly belched gas, ash, and sometimes fiery lava. People in nearby towns keep a close watch on this dangerous mountain.

Popocatépetl

Acapulco, one of Mexico's most popular tourist spots.

Much of Mexico is warm year-round, but the climate varies as much as the land. Coastal lowlands can be hot and steamy. Yucatán and other coastal regions get lots of rain, especially from May to September. Hurricanes may strike along either coast.

Mountain regions are cooler, and the Central Plateau is dry. Especially in the north, land must be irrigated for crops to grow. The southern part of the plateau gets more rain than the north. Mexico City has a pleasant climate, with mild temperatures throughout the year.

With such variety in land and climate, Mexico is home to a great range of wildlife. Deer, coyotes, wolves, and bears live in the mountains and cool northern regions. Jaguars, ocelots, tapirs, and monkeys roam the tropical forests. Parrots, macaws, and brightly colored hummingbirds dart through the rain forest branches.

YOUNG EXPLORER

Can you find Baja California on the map (page 86)?

Underneath the land, Mexico has huge reserves of oil. The country ranks fifth in the world in oil production. It also has copper, zinc, and other minerals—especially gold and silver. Today, Mexico is one of the world's top producers of silver. Centuries ago, it was gold and silver that brought Europeans to this part of the world.

EUROPEANS ARRIVE

The first known people to inhabit what is now Mexico were early tribes around 10,000 B.C. Around 5000 B.C, they began to grow crops and raise animals for food. As their lives changed from wandering to permanent settlement, they built large empires. By A.D. 1500, the Aztecs ruled most of Mexico. Their empire was centered in Tenochtitlan, where Mexico City is today. The Aztec capital was a large city, with canals, squares, temples, and palaces.

In 1519, the Spanish explorer Hernando Cortés reached Mexico. To the Aztecs, the arrival of the Spanish seemed to fulfill a prophecy. This prophecy said that a god known as the Plumed Serpent (Quetzalcoatl) would return to Mexico. The Spanish, with

This illustration depicts Cortés invading Mexico on horseback.

Aztec ruins at Tenochititlán.

their plumed helmets and strange pale faces, fit the story. The Aztecs welcomed them. It's said that the Aztec emperor Montezuma II even invited Cortés to his palace.

It didn't take the Aztecs long to realize that Cortés only wanted gold and silver. They tried to drive the Spanish out. The Spanish had guns and horses, and they crushed the Indians. In addition, many Aztecs were killed by smallpox, a disease brought by the Spanish.

Spain ruled Mexico for three centuries. New Spain, as the colony was called, was a

rich source of silver. Spanish landowners grew wealthy growing sugarcane, wheat, and rice, and raising cattle and sheep. Indians provided the labor for mines, farms, and ranches.

Catholic priests founded missions to convert the Indians to Christianity. They made little progress at first. In time, Spanish settlers and Indians began to marry. As the races blended, so did the cultures. **Mestizos**—people of mixed Spanish and Indian descent—became the largest group in the country. Roman Catholicism became the leading religion. Spanish became the language spoken by almost everyone.

INDEPENDENCE

Mexico's fight for independence from Spain began in 1810. The first leader of the struggle was Miguel Hidalgo y Costilla, a priest. When he called for revolt, mestizos and Indians flocked to support him. Hidalgo was captured and put to death in 1811. Others

Think About It

How have Mexico's natural resources affected its history?

Focus On: Palenque

The ruins of Palenque are hidden in the rain forest of southern Mexico. They are a silent reminder of the glory of ancient Maya civilization. Palenque's pyramids, palaces, and temples date from about A.D. 600 to 800. Many are decorated with stone carvings. The tallest structure is the Temple of Inscriptions, a pyramid with 69 steps. It guards the underground tomb of the Mayan king Pacal, who ruled from 603 to 683.

Palenque

continued the fight. In 1821, Spain finally granted Mexico its freedom.

Independence did not bring peace. Mexico went through a long struggle to become the nation that it is today. First an army officer, Agustín de Iturbide, seized power and declared himself emperor. He was overthrown in 1824, and Mexico became a republic.

Cancun, on Mexico's southern peninsula.

Antonio López de Santa Anna, who became president in 1833, was the most important leader of the era. Rivalry between political groups kept the country weak. Mexico lost Texas to a rebellion. It fought off a French invasion in 1838. In a war with the United States, from 1846 to 1848, it lost New Mexico and California.

In 1855, reformers turned Santa Anna out of office. Led by Benito Juárez, a Zapotec Indian, they set limits on the power of the army and the Church. They also called for freedom of religion, freedom of the press, and other basic rights.

The army, the church, and wealthy landowners opposed these reforms. Civil war broke out. The reformers won, but the fight bankrupted the country. The government was forced to stop payments on debts owed to foreign nations. This led to a French invasion. In 1863, a French army captured Mexico City.

The French sent Archduke Maximilian of Austria to govern Mexico as emperor. He didn't rule long. France was pressured by the United States to end its occupation of Mexico. In 1866, French troops were pulled out. Without their protection, Maximilian was captured and executed in 1867.

THE STRUGGLE FOR REFORM

Juárez once again became president. He continued his reforms. Among the most important was a system of free public schools. Many of Juarez's reforms were undone after his death in 1872.

Porfirio Díaz seized power in 1876. He ruled Mexico as a dictator for nearly 35 years. His rule was harsh, but it brought some good. Díaz built railroads, founded Mexico's oil industry, and brought foreign investment to Mexico. Wealthy landowners, the army, and the Church regained their old powers. Profits went to a few, while workers in cities and on farms lived in poverty.

The result was the Mexican Revolution of 1910. It was led by Pancho Villa, a former bandit, and Emiliano Zapata, a champion of the Indians. The revolution forced Díaz from office in 1911, but Mexico's troubles were not over. Rival leaders struggled for control.

Under Venustiano Carranza, who became president in 1914, Villa and Zapata rebelled again. United States even stepped into the fight, to support Carranza. In 1915, the U.S. Cavalry entered Mexico in pursuit of Villa. He had raided a New Mexico border town. The Cavalry was not successful. Villa had escaped.

Carranza's greatest accomplishment was the Constitution of 1917. This constitution guaranteed public education, gave workers the right to strike, and limited the power of the Church. It gave the government the

Above and right: A variety of scenes in Mexico City, the capital of Mexico.

power to redistribute land. It is said that minerals below the ground, such as oil, belonged to the nation, not to any individual or company.

Most of these reforms were not put into practice right away. In time, many big estates were broken up, and the land was given to poor farmers. In 1938, Mexico's oil industry was nationalized, or taken over, by the government.

The Constitution of 1917 also set up the basic form of government that Mexico has today. Like the United States, Mexico is a republic. Its government has three branches. The executive branch is headed by the president, who is elected for a six-year term. The Congress is the national legislature. It has two houses: the Senate, with members elected for six years, and the Chamber of Deputies, elected for three years. The courts, or judiciary, make up the third branch of government.

MEXICO TODAY

Recent years have brought better living conditions to Mexico. As a result, Mexico's population has soared. Today, Mexico has more people than any other Spanish-speaking country. Mestizos still make up the majority. About 30 percent of the people are of pure Indian descent. About 15 percent are of European ancestry.

Some Indians still live in remote villages in the mountains or near the southern border. Since the 1950s, most Mexicans have left rural areas for cities, searching for a better life. Today, more than 70 percent of the people live in cities. Cities along the U.S. border have grown as U.S. companies have opened factories there. Coastal towns such as Acapulco have become international beach resorts.

A fourth of the people live in and around Mexico City, the capital. It is the second-most-populated city in the world. Mexico City has a lively mixture of old and new, with Spanish colonial buildings and modern skyscrapers. It is home to the National Autonomous University of Mexico. Founded in 1551, this is the oldest university in North America.

Mexico faces many challenges. Air and water pollution are serious problems in Mexico City. Drug trafficking and government corruption trouble the country. The Institutional Revolutionary Party, or PRI,

YOUNG EXPLORER

How has Mexico's long border with the United States affected its history?

A Mexican boy returns home with fish he caught.

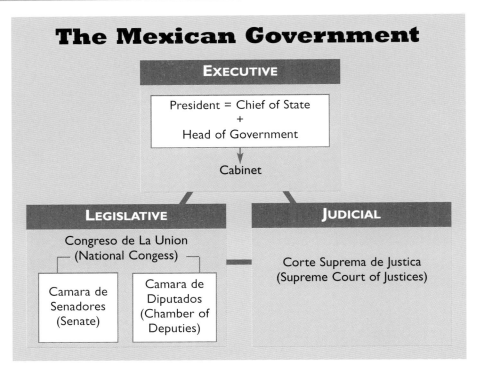

The Mexican Government

EXECUTIVE

President = Chief of State
+
Head of Government

↓

Cabinet

LEGISLATIVE

Congreso de La Union
(National Congess)

Camara de Senadores (Senate)

Camara de Diputados (Chamber of Deputies)

JUDICIAL

Corte Suprema de Justica
(Supreme Court of Justices)

has dominated the government since the 1930s. Faced with growing criticism, government leaders introduced some reforms in the 1990s. The reforms were intended to make Mexico a true democracy, with fair and honest elections.

There are still great gaps between rich and poor in Mexico. A handful of wealthy people live in fine houses with many servants. The poor live in shantytowns around the cities or in rural areas. Many of the poorest Mexicans are Indians. In the 1990s, Indians in Chiapas state, in the south, rebelled and demanded better treatment.

At the same time, Mexico faced a financial crisis. The country had built up huge foreign debts and could not make payments on them. The United States helped arrange a $50 billion rescue package.

Mexican leaders have focused on building up the economy as a way to solve these problems. Oil is still important, but Mexico has many industries today. In 1993, Mexico signed the North American Free Trade Agreement (NAFTA). This treaty lowered barriers to trade with the United States and Canada.

Mexico is favored with rich natural resources, great beauty, and a colorful heritage. Despite its problems, these advantages give the nation a promising future.

CHAPTER REVIEW

1. How does Mexico compare to the United States in size?
2. Where is Mexico's highest mountain?
3. What is Mexico's most important mineral resource?
4. What people ruled Mexico when the

 Think About It

How has rapid population growth helped create some of the problems Mexico faces today?

Spanish first arrived?

5. Who are the mestizos?

6. When did Mexico gain independence from Spain?

7. Who led the Mexican Revolution of 1910?

8. How does Mexico City compare in size to other cities worldwide?

9. In what part of Mexico did Indians rebel in the 1990s?

10. What natural advantages may help Mexico grow in the future?

Activities

Here is a list of some famous Mexicans. Choose a subject for a brief report. Explain what your subject did and why he or she was important.

FLORES DE ANDRADE, Revolutionary women's organizer

LÁZARO CÁRDENAS, Mexican president

BARTOLOMÉ DE LAS CASAS, Missionary priest

HERNANDO CORTÉS, Spanish explorer

CARLOS FUENTES, Author

MIGUEL HIDALGO Y COSTILLA, Revolutionary leader

SOR JUANA (JUANA INÉS DE LA CRUZ), Scholar and nun

BENITO JUÁREZ, Reformer and president

MAXIMILIAN I (MAXIMILIAN OF AUSTRIA), Mexican emperor

JOSEFA ORTIZ DE DOMÍNGUEZ, Revolutionary heroine

OCTAVIO PAZ, Poet and Nobel Prize winner

DIEGO RIVERA, painter

ANTONIO LÚPEZ DE SANTA ANNA, Military and political leader

PANCHO VILLA, Revolutionary leader

EMILIANO ZAPATA, Revolutionary leader

FOCUS ON: Celebrating Mexico

National holidays, religious holidays, and local traditions are celebrated with fiestas in most Mexican cities and towns. Here are just a few of these events. Choose one to research. Then write a short report.

Cinco de Mayo
May 5, nationwide

Corpus Christi Day
June, Papantla

Day of the Dead
November 1, nationwide

Day of the Virgin of Guadalupe
December 12, Mexico City and elsewhere

Flower Fair
Cuernavaca, April

Day of the Virgin of Charity and Assumption Day
Huamantia, August

Independence Day
September 16, Dolores Hidalgo and nationwide

Night of the Radishes
December 23, Oaxaca

Glossary

abolitionist A person who wants to end, or abolish, slavery.

amendment A change, such as a change to the U.S. Constitution.

archaeologist A person who studies the remains of ancient civilizations.

Arctic Circle An imaginary line that encloses the northern polar region. The line circles the globe at about 66 1/2 degrees north latitude.

badlands Land carved into strange shapes by wind and water.

barrier island A long island that lies parallel to the coast and protects the coast from ocean winds and waves.

boomtown A town that springs up and grows fast during economic good times.

clan A group of people who share common ancestors.

colony A settlement in new territory, founded by people from another land and governed by the parent country.

compass An instrument or symbol for finding directions.

constitutional monarchy A government in which a king or queen is head of state but has little or no power.

continent One of Earth's seven great landmasses.

democratic system A system in which people control their government.

direction The way someone or something is pointing.

diversified Varied.

east One of the four main points of the compass, and the direction in which the sun rises.

equator An imaginary line around the middle of the earth, halfway between the North and South Poles.

ethnic Having to do with race and culture. Member of an ethnic group may share a racial, cultural, national, or tribal background. They often speak the same language and follow the same religion and traditions.

federal system A system in which power is shared by a central government and state or provincial governments.

fertile Productive. Fertile soil is good for growing crops.

glacier A massive sheet of ice that spreads over land.

gorge A deep chasm or canyon.

homesteaders Pioneers who settled on the Great Plains in the 1800s.

hydroelectric power Electricity produce by waterpower.

immigrant A person who comes to live in a country.

indentured servant A person who is bound by contract to work for another for a set period of time.

irrigated Artificially watered. Irrigation systems bring water to dry places so that crops can grow.

land bridge A strip of land joining two larger landmasses.

latitude The position of a place, measured in degrees north or south of the equator.

longitude The position of a place, measured in degrees east or west of a line that runs through Greenwich, England.

map key A key that explains the symbols on a map.

mesa An isolated hill or mountain with steep sides and a flat top.

mestizos People of mixed Spanish and Native American descent.

metropolitan area A region that includes a city and, often, surrounding suburbs.

migrant A person who moves from place to place.

militia Citizen soldiers, generally called to serve in emergencies.

missionary A person who is sent abroad to spread a religious faith.

natural resources map Map that shows the natural resources of an area, such as minerals.

north One of four main points on a compass. It is toward the North Pole.

Northern Hemisphere The half of the Earth that is above (north of) the equator.

permafrost Permanently frozen ground.

plateau A broad region of high, mostly level ground.

political map Map that shows the capital cities, big cities, and the borders between countries.

population density map Map that shows the population of an area.

prairie A grass-covered plain.

pueblos Multi-family dwellings built by Indians of the Southwest.

rain forest A forest that gets an exceptional amount of rain, often 100 inches or more in a year.

representative democracy A system in which people elect officials to run the government.

reservation An area set aside for a Native American group.

segregation Separation. Segregation laws once separated black and white Americans in housing, education, and other areas of life.

sharecroppers Tenant farmers who give a share of their crop as rent for the land they farm.

south One of the four main points of a compass. It is toward the South Pole.

Southern Hemisphere The half of the Earth that is below (south of) the equator.

temperate Moderate.

topographical map Map that shows an area's natural features, such as jungles, deserts, and mountains.

tributary A river that flows into a larger river.

tundra Treeless plains of the far north.

west One of the four main points of the compass, and the direction in which the sun sets.

For More Information

Further Reading

Bock, Judy. Scholastic *Encyclopedia of the United States*. New York, NY: Scholastic Trade, 1997.

Gresko, Marcia S. *Canada (Letters Home From)*. Woodbridge, CT: Blackbirch Press, Inc., 2000.

Gresko, Marcia S. *Mexico (Letters Home From)*. Woodbridge, CT: Blackbirch Press, Inc., 1999.

Miller, Millie. *The United States of America: A State-By-State Guide*. New York, NY: Scholastic Trade, 1999.

Petersen, David. *North America (True Book)*. Danbury, CT: Children's Press, 1998.

Quiri, Patricia Ryon. *The Constitution (True Book)*. Danbury, CT: Children's Press, 1998.

Ricciuti, Edward. *America's Top 10 Natural Wonders*. Woodbridge, CT: Blackbirch Press, Inc., 1998.

Sobel, Syl. *How the U.S. Government Works*. Hauppauge, NY: Barrons Juveniles, 1999.

Tesar, Jenny. *America's Top 10 Cities*. Woodbridge, CT: Blackbirch Press, Inc., 1998.

Wood, Marion. *The World of Native Americans (The World of)*. New York, NY: Peter Bedrick Books, 1997.

CD-ROMs

United States Geography. Fogware Publishing.

Where In The U.S.A. Is Carmen Sandiego. The Learning Company.

Videos

Just the Facts: The Great American State Quiz. Goldhil Home Media, 1999.

Just the Facts: United States Constitution. Goldhil Home Media, 1999.

Mexico: A Story of Courage and Conquest. New Video Group, 1999.

Really Wild Animals: Amazing North America. National Geographic Kids Video, 1994.

Surprises of the Great White North: Alaska and Canada (Amazing Wonders of the World). Questar, Inc., 1999.

Touring Canada's National Parks. Questar, Inc., 1996.

Web Sites

Alabama www.state.al.us/
Alaska www.state.ak.us/
Arizona www.state.az.us/
Arkansas www.state.ar.us/
California www.state.ca.us/
Canada www.canada.gc.ca/
Colorado www.state.co.us/
Connecticut www.state.ct.us/
Delaware www.state.de.us/
Florida www.myflorida.com/
Georgia www.state.ga.us/
Hawaii www.state.hi.us/
Idaho www.state.id.us/
Illinois www.state.il.us/
Indiana www.state.in.us/
Iowa www.state.ia.us/
Kansas www.state.ks.us/
Kentucky www.state.ky.us/
Louisiana www.state.la.us/
Maine www.state.me.us/
Maryland www.mec.state.md.us/
Massachusetts www.state.ma.us/
Mexico http://world.presidencia.gob.mx/pages/frames/f_government.html
Michigan www.state.mi.us/
Minnesota www.state.mn.us/
Mississippi www.state.ms.us/
Missouri www.state.mo.us/
Montana www.state.mt.us/
Nebraska www.state.ne.us/
Nevada www.state.nv.us/
New Hampshire www.state.nh.us/
New Jersey www.state.nj.us/
New Mexico www.state.nm.us/
New York www.state.ny.us/
North Carolina www.ncgov.com/
North Dakota www.discovernd.com/
Ohio www.state.oh.us/
Oklahoma www.state.ok.us
Oregon www.state.or.us/
Pennsylvania www.state.pa.us
Rhode Island www.state.ri.us/
South Carolina www.state.sc.us
South Dakota www.state.sd.us/
Tennessee www.state.tn.us/
Texas www.state.tx.us/
Utah www.state.ut.us/
Vermont www.state.vt.us/
Virginia www.state.va.us/
Washington www.access.wa.gov/
West Virginia www.state.wv.us/
Wisconsin www.state.wi.us/
Wyoming www.state.wy.us/

Index